'*Encyclopaedia of Snow* aims high, and .... kinds of risk-taking . . . There is a crystal of strong intent at the heart of its snowflake construction . . . With sensitivity and wit, Miano explores the many-sidedness of a thing, the unpinnable quality of our hearts, the layers between presentation and meaning . . . [She is] a writer of great intelligence'
Emily Perkins, *Independent*

'Science, history, myth and fabrication are interleaved with a number of love stories . . . By not filling in the gaps, Miano evokes emotions and displays considerable literary sensibility and talent'
Amanda Craig, *The Times*

'As its narrative unfolds, it slowly becomes a missive of love. A cool and ambitious start'
Susan Corrigan, *I-D*

'This is in part a study of alchemy, a snow-demonology of angels and apparitions, legendary winter spirits and Inuit sprites, all flickering in an ethereal half-light. Impeccably researched, *Encyclopaedia of Snow* is a bravura display of smoke-and-mirrors trickery'
Alastair Sooke, *Sunday Telegraph*

'A delicate work, as poetic as it is erudite'
Hermione Eyre, *Independent on Sunday*

'Miano is enigmatic in a myth-making way'
Victoria Lane, *Daily Telegraph*

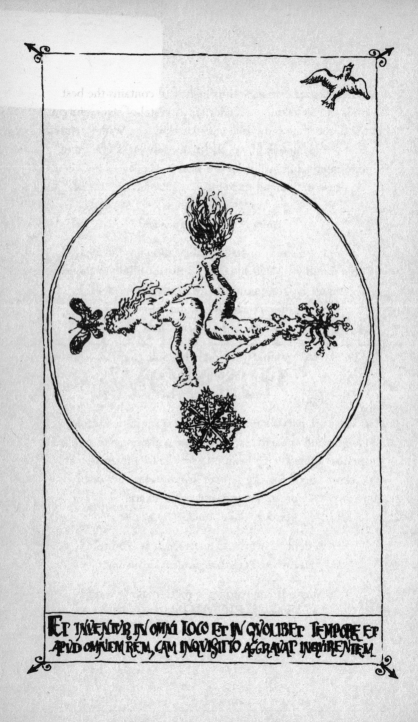

ET INVENITVR IN OMNI LOCO ET IN QVOLIBET TEMPORE ET
APVD OMNEM REM, CAM INQVISITIO AGGRAVAT INQVIRENTEM.

SARAH EMILY MIANO

❄

ENCYCLOPÆDIA OF SNOW

PICADOR

First published 2003 by Picador

This paperback edition published 2004 by Picador
an imprint of Pan Macmillan Ltd
Pan Macmillan, 20 New Wharf Road, London N1 9RR
Basingstoke and Oxford
Associated companies throughout the world
www.panmacmillan.com

ISBN 0 330 41178 0

3 5 7 9 8 6 4 2

A CIP catalogue record for this book is available from
the British Library.

Printed and bound in Great Britain by
Mackays of Chatham plc, Chatham, Kent

For W. G. Sebald

The publishers gratefully acknowledge permission to
reproduce copyright material from:

'A Winter's Tale' by Dylan Thomas
published in *Deaths and Entrances*, 1946,
reprinted by permission of The Dylan Thomas Estate
and David Higham Associates;

Ways of Seeing, 1972, by John Berger,
reprinted by permission of Penguin Books Ltd.

Every effort has been made to trace the copyright holders
but if any have been inadvertently overlooked the publishers
will be pleased to make the necessary arrangement
at the first opportunity.

The author would like to acknowledge that 'Polar-ity'
is an adaptation of A. S. Byatt's short story, 'Cold',
published in *Elementals*, 1999.

Prologue

CITY UNDER SIEGE BY SNOWSTORM

THE BUFFALO DAILY NEWS, *December 12, 2000, 9 a.m.*

BUFFALO, N.Y. – Buffalo got hammered Sunday by a savage lake-effect snowstorm that dumped 37 inches in 6 hours, one of the heaviest snowfalls it has ever seen in one day since the renowned Blizzard of 1977.

The second-largest storm in the city's history moved in at 4 p.m. and dropped more than 3 feet of new snow on top of the record totals on the ground before Monday, 6 a.m., shutting down streets, offices and the International airport.

Suburban or remote areas surrounding Lake Erie confronted more than 6 feet, according to the National Weather Service's airport measuring station.

Thousands of Buffalonians waited overnight in stranded automobiles on the highways, while the city streets were in a gridlock. Mayor Anthony Masiello declared a State of Emergency and assembled road crews and snowplows to rescue stranded drivers. Western New York plow drivers who had been waiting for work found the going rough. "One wrong move on these streets and you're stuck for good," said Ed Krekowski, owner of Ed's Garage on Chippewa Street.

Meanwhile, Mayor Masiello urged motorists to stay away from the city. "It's a labyrinth out there," he said.

Meteorologist Fred Frigowsky said large masses of cold air were siphoning moisture from Lake Erie and dropping it in bands of snow. "These bands keep going back and forth, back and forth," Frigowsky said.

Pedestrians struggled through chest-high drifts. Resident Marsha McElhanney tried shoveling through blockades of snow in her driveway when she stayed home from work. "I couldn't see my front door from the sidewalk. It looked like white static, like we were hit by an avalanche."

A man was killed early Sunday when his Pontiac Sunbird struck a pickup truck on a highway in Tonawanda, Erie County. The accident occurred at approximately 12 p.m. on the I-190 into the city of Buffalo. He was pronounced dead at the scene. The accident closed the I-190 to traffic for nearly four hours.

"So, we had a good fall and a great summer anyway, ya know? Whaddya gonna do?" said Joey Sorrento, working the takeout counter at his pizza parlor.

Witnesses to the accident on the I-190 please call the Tonawanda police at (716) 694-6000.

Editor's Note

Dear Reader,

I, too, see him everywhere, in my own reflection in a train window, as flashes of white in a crowd, a figure of blue in the twilight. He alters, for me, with each circumstance. But will I ever know how much he haunts you; and whether, in between the sightings, you also hear his stories? Did you ever hear them? Stories he'd gathered on his travels, through the Alps, the Apennines, the Arctic Circle – stories plucked from friends I'd never meet, the ones he said were like us, obsessed with snow, outside time even.

Did you know there is a lake of cold on the moon, as well as a sea of pain? he'd asked early on; and after a silence, I listened as he began his first story with his first cigarette, pulling each extract from memory in a seemingly random order, speaking in voices as if possessed by strange spirits. Carefully, throughout the months, I observed the growth of something extraordinary from this collection of stories, which I could not define, but began like a tiny crystal and became a snowflake with many tendrils and sprigs.

Editor's Note

Little did I realize, or you realize, that the stories he shared were the makings of a life's work; an assemblage of clippings, quotes, photographs, notes, jokes, anecdotes, poems, songs; and contained in something like a scrapbook, kept under lock and key, wholly dedicated to the one thing that is most forgetful.

Editor, Buffalo, N.Y.

ANGEL, a cherub, seraph, archangel, divine messenger; a well-known example Gabriel, who appeared to the Virgin Mary, informing her that she would have a son. An angel may also be an imprint left behind in the snow. Other times it is represented with wings and arrayed in white. Very rarely, an angel is blue like me, and poses for dirty post-cards. When I first met Mut, he came backstage after my performance at the Club. I was scanty in my bloomers. He told me I sang his favourite song, 'Falling in Love Again,' in a helpless way. 'Just like an angel,' he said. 'Can't help it,' I replied. 'What am I to do?' Mut removed his spectacles and got down on his knees with the dirty handkerchiefs and sheet music. 'Why do you work in a place like this?' he asked. 'Well . . . It's an art, isn't it,' I said, 'to make something out of life?' He helped me put on my stockings, then brushed my hair and said, 'You're really sweet.' 'You must come again tomorrow,' I told him. When he did, Mut crowed like a rooster and dressed up as a clown simply for my amusement. But after I got pregnant and we married, he stopped calling me his angel and seemed to seek shame and humiliation in everything. Eventually, he shut himself in his room and would not speak or eat. Then he lost it: assaulted me while I was embracing Mazeppa the Strong Man. The crowd turned into an angry mob that dragged my husband off and beat him. Most likely he escaped – I heard he was seen entering his school for boys not long after. Poor Mut, he was such a blustery professor.

See PROMISE   *Lola-Lola, Germany*

❄

BLINDNESS is a loss of sight that can be caused by over-exposure of the eye to ultraviolet rays reflected from the snow. Usually the cornea absorbs ultraviolet rays but under conditions of increased exposure, its protective mechanism conks out.*

Please, by all means, wear dark-coloured glasses when you're out in the snow. It is unpleasant when your eyes are inflamed and you have to stay indoors for weeks, fearing the light. I'd been trudging in the snow that winter afternoon with my sad sheepdog named Burns, both eager for a pee,

---

* When the eye encounters a bright light the photo-pigments of the retina are bleached, which stimulates the receptors (the number of which is approximately the same as the population of Greater New York). When the eye adjusts to the light the retina fires a positive afterimage, which looks like a dark shape hovering in space.

when I realized we'd cleared a path for ourselves all the way into an open field, surrounded by undulating hills of bright snow. Our tracks, tiny dots of brown from the muddy underneath, were hardly visible behind us. Burns barked just as I got blinking, batting my wet eyelashes in vain and seeing nothing. The snow's light slashed at my eyes, bored a hole in me and grabbed me by the innards. I saw a dark shape hovering in space, then I was sucked up from my space where my two feet had been planted in snow, vacuumed into a black hole, swirled and spat back into my suede boots. Blinded, I staggered and toppled over. I lay there in the snow for a while, limbs splayed, but I could not move.

Meanwhile, Burns lifted his left leg and piddled in the snow. After he was done he bit into my wool coat at the sleeve and tugged at me. Grrrr, Burns said. Grrrr, Grrr! I replied. Still, I couldn't see. It was getting colder. Using Burns's large frame, I propped myself up on two feet and then we began to walk. My left hand grazed his back as we did, while I kept my eyes closed and shielded them (for added security) with my other hand. We reached our cottage at Sleat. I fumbled with the key for five minutes and we went inside. I made a fire, blindly, crawled in bed under a blanket and lay there for days.

See FIBS OF VISION　　　*Sandy Cumming, Isle of Skye*

Further reading: Whittier, John Greenleaf, "Snow-Bound" from *A Winter Idyl*, Boston, 1866.

COMETS and meteors are called faeces of stars, according to the Nunamiut Eskimos, but the Kiliwa believe that meteors are, in actuality, the fiery urine of the constellation Xsmii. It's not easy to define these bits of stuff that orbit through our solar system, but how could scientists believe that a comet* is a "flying sandbank"? What a ridiculous thought! It is obvious that a comet is a giant, dirty snowball, with a solid center of ice, ammonia, methane, carbon dioxide, hydrogen cyanide and mineral dusts, and a fuzzy part around it like a vapor cloud. Then, when the comet gets close to the sun, the ice vaporizes and it grows two tails, creating a storm of falling stars, sometimes speeding up fast enough to propel the comet around the sun in one day, like an ice-skater cracking the whip.

See ICE   *F. L. Whipple, Iowa*

❄

CRYSTALS of snow are formed in the atmosphere at a freezing temperature ($-40°C$) by condensation of water vapour on a *condensation nucleus* or tiny ice crystal. Condensation occurs when water vapour changes to ice, skipping the liquid state and the process of sublimation. When water droplets are in a supercooled state and in the presence of

---

* A comet is interpreted as an omen of catastrophe. Its arrival is often sudden and unexpected.

ice crystals, they evaporate and freeze on to the nuclei. The crystals individually collect molecules of vapour one at a time, building into a hexagonal pattern until transparent, beautifully intricate like a spider's web. Upon reaching the ground, crystals lose shape and become granular in form due to evaporation and condensation. Rimelike ice crystals or *pogonip*, a Shoshone word for 'white death,' form in a freezing fog, then drift in the air so densely they make a tingling sound as they collide. The air instantly fills with flying needles of ice, which adhere to any surface – trees, plants, rocks – to form ice-blossoms or frost-flowers. Snowflakes, then, are clumps of crystals.* When snowflakes unite with other flakes they grow larger. On rare occasions flakes are very large – measuring 15" × 8" – as in Fort Keogh, Montana, in Jan. 1887, when they were 'larger than milk pans.' Even when small – half an inch in diameter – snowflakes can be gathered in your hands or caught on your tongue, with the air at or below freezing temperature.

U. Nakaya, Hokkaido

❄

---

* "The growth of a genuine tradition resembles that of a crystal, which attracts homologous particles to itself, incorporating them according to its own laws of unity" – Titus Burkhardt, 1967.

5

Crystallisation (positive): Austrian salt miners will hurl a leafless bough into an abandoned working and pull it out three months later with a deposit of crystals that resembles a galaxy of stars. Similarly, crystallisation is a mental process that occurs between two lovers. This is what will happen when one lover leaves another alone with his thoughts for a period of time: the one in love will draw from everything new proofs of the perfection in his lover, and will wildly overrate them, as something fallen from Heaven, a crystal.

See POLAR-ITY   *M. H. Beyle, Milan*

❄

Crystallisation (negative): My eyes are dried up like marbles. Sorrows in fiction make me open up and overflow with emotion whilst real sorrows, such as watching my sister Caroline lay dying, remain hard and bitter in my heart after turning to crystal.*

G. Flaubert, Paris

Further reading: Humphreys, Bentley and William Jackson, *Snow Crystals*, London, 1931; Koi, Toshitsura Oinokami Doi,

---

* "There is nothing new on earth / For a person who lives long and experiences much. / In my years of youthful wandering / I have seen crystallized people." – Goethe, *Faust*.

Sekka Zusetsu (Illustration of Snow Blossoms), Japan, 1833; Hellman, Gustav, *Schneekrystalle,* Germany, 1893.

❆

DARKNESS, a blackness, gloom, concealment. I am struck by the impression that darkness has a direct correlation to the sensation of cold. Positively it does! One night I went to the theatre in Paris to see a performance of *Esther*, sitting in my usual box at the usual time, nearly eight o'clock. Immediately I noticed it was very dark inside, as the lone candelabrum did not provide enough light for the entire theatre and I sat in the balcony. The performance began with the introduction of Esther, the daughter of Ab'ihail, the uncle of Mor'decai, visiting the royal house of King Ahasue'rus. Soon, as Esther denounced the bad man, Haman, I noticed the theatre grew colder. Then, when Haman threw himself at Esther's feet, requesting for his soul – yes, at this moment exactly – I entered a world of darkness. Significantly, as I went deeper into this black cave, the tips of my fingers began to freeze. I felt as if I had plunged all of them deep into a bucket of ice. Eventually they were positively frostbitten. I found it rather odd to notice other people nearby, in lighter clothing, wiping their brows and fanning their faces. Meanwhile, the coldness spread through my veins as streaks of great pleasure. This cold became alarming, but I was curious to know whether it would continue and so I waited. Soon I was a statue carved of ice, all my thoughts of ice.*

Charles-Pierre Baudelaire, Paris

❅

DEATHS AND ENTRANCES:

After years of having and dumping this girl or that girl, Cousin Tony had finally found "the one." What a relief. The whole family was fed up with trying to remember each new girlfriend's name and then getting the evil eye from Tony when we used the wrong one. Then Valeria came along, followed by fireworks et al., and a sudden invitation for a wedding held in the dead of winter at Our Lady of Perpetual Help, or just "Our Lady," as we regulars called it.

Today was the day.

My family sat in the pews on the right side of the church along with the rest of the Guerriris – row after row of Italian smiles. Outside the double doors a steeple pierced the grey cloud above the city. Inside the double doors a bold crucifix seemed to hold the whole fortress together.

I brought my best friend Corey as my date because when I first got the invitation, the inside envelope read: "Stella

---

* Like the black and white halves of the Ouroboros – a symbol of unity – dark and light are antinomies (opposites which complement one another), as is true of hot and cold, love and hate, life and death.

and guest." I was shocked! *Me? A date?* But I guess the family thought that fourteen was the perfect time to start "getting busy," so Corey sat on my right side, awkward in his little brother's shiny black suit and skinny black tie that landed too far below his belt buckle. On the other side was Mama, then Papa, who leaned forward periodically to wink at me. My little sister and brother, Fran and Louie, squirmed around, sometimes hitting each other on Corey's right. Apparently it was *my* job to keep watch over them, a task, with Corey's help, that required their constant feeding and watering, like my gerbils. I glimpsed Grandpa's shiny bald spot surrounded by his blinding white hair when, a few rows up, Auntie Sylvia in a red wig leaned into her pocketbook for more chewing gum. It took more stretching than normal to see Grandpa, though, because he was in the second row behind Cousin Tony's parents. Plus, he didn't stand out as much as he used to – age had been slyly shrinking him.

While everyone waited for the ceremony to begin – giving sideways hellos and trading fidgeting babies – my eyes scanned the white nuptial carpet from the candlelit altar all the way back to the double doors, which usually opened out into the stained city street, but had just been shut by two solemn-faced boys. That's where they would make their entrance, I thought, as I surveyed the back of the church. None of the wedding party were gathered in the back like I suspected they might be, only the altar boys who were now coming forward along the aisle dividing the bride's and groom's families – a prelude to the choir – whose presence made me feel secure in the cosy confines.

I waited for the hush to sweep the crowd. Once they were quiet, I knew the bride would make her entrance and I was anxious to see her. This was the first time the Guerriris would ever see Valeria, who somehow coaxed Tony into settling down. That wasn't the reason I was eager to see her though. I wanted to see what sort of dress she'd wear, full or slinky, what kind of headpiece she'd chosen, a tiara or a wreath, what type of bouquet she'd hold, white lilies or fresh-picked daisies. I wondered what style of dress I might wear when I got married, or if I would ever find someone I loved, and what he would look like. I wondered if he might even turn out to be Corey.

Surreptitiously, I glanced at him. His arms were stretched behind him as he attempted to wiggle out of the tiny suit jacket. It must have been caught on his watch because it wasn't coming off. Mama reached across to help then, when the tugging was over and the jacket was off, he sat there slumped in a paper-thin, white shirt. Obviously he didn't know to wear a T-shirt underneath, or anti-perspirant. His nipples poked from beneath the shirt; and when he lifted his arm to drape it behind me, he had two wet rings circling his armpits all the way down to his mid-torso. I was mortified! Flushed, I looked away with the answer to my question.

The choir of twelve began singing and one of the men sang in a baritone that made me swoon. I closed my eyes and breathed in the smell of incense. I wrapped my arms around my front, clutching my sides, as the harpist caressed her strings. Off to the right the organ player swayed on his bench. It was the most heart-pumping rendition of "Ave Maria" that I'd ever heard. It surprised me how happy I could be, sitting uncomfortably in the rigid pew and not talking to Corey much.

Then the hush and all eyes focused on the aisle, awaiting the appearance of the wedding party: the Guerriri side looked to the left, the bride's side to the right. A Mozart sinfonia concertante cued Cousin Tony the groom and his men to walk the aisle, which they did in their typical feet-pointing-outward, Italian-stallion strut. It had a casualness that felt out of place for both the wedding and the music. Corey giggled, so I knew he agreed. Then the organ struck a glorious loud chord and the harpist's notes chimed in, playing pizzicato and sounding peculiarly violin-like. The chords fell upon me like rain until they faded into a brief pause and started up again with Mozart's Symphony no. 25.

It was time.

I leaned far over into the aisle for a near-perfect glimpse. The bride emerged, arrayed in white poof, beads and frill, and a taffeta train that streaked for miles as she journeyed slowly toward her groom. She was beautiful. Her face was hidden beneath the veil, but she had long, dark hair that was swept in a bouffant with a sparkling tiara. The rest tumbled in curls. The lilies sprinkled with baby's breath shook slightly in her hands. Her father, in tails, escorted her chest up-and-out and eyes scanning the crowd. When Valeria paused in the aisle for the photographer's flash at the point level with us, I spotted an accessory I hadn't noticed before. Hmmm. Tony had been a busy man in the eight months since the two initially met. For Valeria's belly protruded up and out, enough for everyone to recognize that another Guerriri was on the way! I sighed, and others gasped. Then Valeria continued on and met Cousin Tony at the front. Her father gave her away to her groom, who smiled and winked.

After a few introductions and brief comments by Father Bob, who would perform the ceremony, Cousin Rosie, Tony's sister, was summoned from the front row to give her blessings to the couple and recite a Bible passage: "Charity suffereth long, and is kind; charity envieth not; charity vaunteth not itself." The words whistled through her horse-like teeth and stumbled across her large bottom lip in a typical West-Side tone. Cousin Rosie continued her pithy reassurance to the new couple by reading the account of true lovers, Ruth and Boaz. I leaned forward to listen closely. It was my favorite. Boaz awakes one night to discover a woman lying down at his feet, and he asks her who she is because he can't see her in the dark. She tells him she is Ruth, his slave girl, and he tells her that she is an excellent woman. Then he gives Ruth a bunch of barley, takes her as his wife, and later she bears him a son named Obed. As I listened to the story, Corey's presence next to me grew heavier, but I didn't glance over, fearful he would look back.

After the story, Rosie gave a brief tribute to Father Bob, who, she said, acted as her "shepherd and protector" in her teenage years. I wondered how that could be. Father Bob was no Pit Bull. He was a coarse-haired man who most resembled a Chihuahua, and I couldn't see him protecting anyone. He walked with a bothersome slouch and when he looked, he stared through beady green eyes. With long rubbery arms, his hands almost touched the floor. Despite Rosie's melodrama, Father Bob didn't flinch throughout the speech. I think he was inhaling too much of the incense. Rosie paused and faced her brother Tony and her future sister-in-law Valeria, who, as Mama pointed out, across my lap, was well into her fourth month. "To love nothing is to be nothing," Rosie concluded.

At that word and glance, a beam of sunlight streamed through the stained glass and enlightened the crucifix in a rainbow of colors. The arched spectrum spread over the baby lamb that was cradled in the Lord's arms. The sunlight made Rosie's black hair take on a deep purple. My face turned red with excitement and I looked around. Grandpa planted a kiss on my step-grandma Sandra's cheek. Rosie dried her dewy eyelashes with the edges of her fingers and,

with a joyful sniffle, returned to her place in the brides-
maids' line. Valeria rubbed her stomach. Tony gave his sister
a way-to-go fist. Everyone was smiling, including Corey.

When Tony and Valeria started lighting the candles I
wished I'd sat up front next to Grandpa. Some lonely
years after Grandma Guerriri died and before Grandpa
remarried, his porcelain-top kitchen table became an altar
of assorted wax candles that burned for hours, dripping
and hardening on to the tabletop, then gathered up by his
hands and melted again, over and over. The unremitting
cycle and the reflection of the flickering light in his eyes
entranced me. I never met Grandma Guerriri. She died of
cancer when my parents were first married and before they
had kids. So my love for her was only from second-hand
experience, from nights when I visited Grandpa and gazed
at him surrounded by his entourage of candles while he
brought insights and answers. "Grandma used to do that all
the time when she was worried," he said when I twirled my
hair with my finger. "She loved reading books more than
anything, and she loved crossword puzzles." Me too.

Cameras flashed to signal the start of the vows. Clumsily
the bride and groom exchanged rings. "I now pronounce
you—" Father Bob began, but was suddenly interrupted as
Tony lunged for Valeria, grabbed her in a warm embrace
and smooched her uncontrollably. "—man-n-wife you may
now kiss the bride!" Father Bob finished, and raised his
hands in a cue to the crowd of Catholics who knew just what

to do: guests turned right, left, back and every-which-way to smack their neighbor. This time, on holy ground, it was the smacking of lips. There were a few embraces, handshakes and rear pats thrown in too. I don't know if it was fear of intimacy or a sweat repulsion that seized me, but when Corey leaned over to peck my cheek, I dodged. Instead, Mama caught his kiss but didn't seem to mind.

After the ceremony, all of us, now bundled in muffs and furs, gathered outside on the shoveled walks of Delaware Avenue. I shivered in my overcoat, which didn't warm me much anyway, with its loose liner and missing buttons. As the bride and groom emerged, rice was thrown in arches and landed in the snow. I looked up at the grey sky* and the church, deteriorating but frighteningly potent. "Our Lady."

It was the same church that Papa went to when he was an altar boy, a "scrawny, clumsy, girl-crazy boy," so he always said, and with a "big space between his teeth." He referred to that space as if it was something *of long ago*; and I couldn't understand why, because it was still there. Papa held on to the image of the altar boy by reaching out to the poor boy, struggling family and forgotten old lady. He also walked around with holes in his shoes and toes poking

---

* "The sky, the bird, the bride, / The cloud, the need, the planted stars, the joy beyond / The fields of seed and the time dying flesh astride, / The heavens, the heaven, the grave, the burning font." – Dylan Thomas, 1914–53.

through his socks, like he did as a boy. It was his father, Grandpa Guerriri, who forfeited new shoes or socks for Papa because he wanted to give the neighbors something – a bathtub that drained or a working toilet.

I got rice thrown in my eye and spent the first part of the evening in the bathroom of the fire hall, trying to make the redness go away. I bent over the sink and splashed cold water at my face. I looked in the mirror with my left eye while I prodded the other injured one, looking for rice remainders. Then, women in pastels and smelling of musk elbowed me to get closer to the mirror. My eye was still sore, so I fought for space awhile, but eventually they crowded me out. I exited and headed toward the wedding feast, bypassing Cousin Rosie being dribbled on by some phony and avoiding conversation regarding my plans for the rest of my life. I spotted Corey across the room, hanging close to my wild cousins and gangster uncles, drinking Chianti.

After a dinner of spaghetti bolognese and chicken cacciatore, Papa, a natural entertainer, was called to the microphone to sing. He belted out "Miracle of Miracles" from *Fiddler on the Roof* and got choked up at the part when he sang, "Out of a worthless lump of clay, God has made a man today." Others cried too, but I didn't.

I tried to get a good view for the cake-cutting part because I wanted to see if Valeria would smash white mush into Tony's face. I weaved through the crowd, then tiptoed behind one of the front tables, where Grandpa sat with

Sandra and my other aunts and uncles. Grandpa had his arm draped around Sandra's shoulders, and they were watching the cake, but somehow he spotted me. He reached through the crowd and grabbed my arm, pulled me on to his lap and pretended to pull a potato out of my ear. I laughed and thought it was so weird that Grandpa carried potatoes on him – even at a wedding, wearing a tuxedo. I couldn't believe that, at one time, I really thought Grandpa had found tubers in my ear. He nudged me to pay attention to the cake-cutting, but I couldn't see a thing with all the flashes taking place. When it was over, Grandpa gave me a big kiss and we said goodbye. Not even old age could make him into a geezer, I thought.

After the Chicken Dance, we piled into our wood-paneled station wagon, which we called "Big Blue." Corey and I sat way back, in the seat that faced the rear window, where we could closely watch the road just traveled. I fixated on the yellow lines so hard it seemed like the car was swerving, and it could've been, because even when Papa wasn't drunk he wasn't such a good driver. I did not want to go home. I wanted Papa to drive somewhere beyond so I could watch the barren, dense trees splash against the blue sky over and over again. Returning home meant the end of what seemed like perfect beauty, back to reality and fewer smiles, back to Mama and Papa's screaming matches and the awkward silences in between.

As we neared home, I lay my head on the vinyl armrest

and closed my eyes. Corey slowly traced my spine with his fingers, but I ignored him, pretending I was asleep. Still, he began forming the letters one-by-one. I-L-O-V-E-Y-O-U. *No, you don't,* I thought. *You don't even know me. You just love my family . . . and that's not me.* Then I really did fall asleep, with Corey's hand still on my back.

When Papa turned into our driveway I awoke with a jolt. All of us piled out of the wagon and into the casa like cattle to the slaughter. Everyone went upstairs, even Corey, who was told to sleep in Louie's room. I keeled over on to the couch in my clothes, dozing. So when the telephone rang one hour later, I picked it up.

"Hullo?"

"It's Sandra."

"Oh, hi!"

She was silent except for a few sniffles and then, when I heard the heaviness in her voice, I held my breath.

"Can I talk to your Papa?"

I sensed it was something serious so I slammed the phone down on the table and took the stairs two-at-a-time.

"Papa! Wake up! Get the phone!"

I heard him scramble for their bedside phone as I knelt before the door, peeking through the open space. Papa sat on the edge of the bed in his white briefs, his bare feet planted on the floor. I saw Mama stirring in the sheets. Papa was mumbling, then his head dropped. His face reddened. Mama sat up and touched his back.

He put the receiver down gently.

"What is it?" she asked.

Papa slumped into her arms. "He's gone. Papa's dead."

I ran into Louie's room and climbed into bed with him. He woke up from the jostling and, after I told him the news, we clutched each other, crying. Corey heard and awoke, and then he joined us, clutching, crying.

Grandpa had had a heart attack in the tub.

He'd gone to the bathroom during the commercials but Sandra noticed it took him a little longer than usual. So when the commercials were over and Bob Hope came back on, she called for him

"Sam!"

"Sam!"

Silence. Then a thud, a sound that came and went quickly, but drowned out even the laughter of Hope's audience. Grandpa had been on the toilet, *Reader's Digest* in hand, and had toppled off the pot into the empty tub.

Somebody had deflated the lifejacket of our family. We'd all expected him to live forever. Even his dogs, the two Boston Terriers, slobbered for weeks. Grandpa was not only the life of the party: he was the Guerriri fortress. He raised us grandkids as his own, with traditions, however unusual. When I was six, Grandpa taught me how to ride a bike. When I was seven, he read my first poem, called "If I Was A Butterfly," and told me he would get it published and make me famous. When I was eight, Grandpa took me on my first Ferris wheel. When I was ten, Grandpa taught me how to smoke. When I was twelve, he taught me to drive his pickup truck with a whole heap of junk banging around in the back. When I turned thirteen he gave me his trusty typewriter.

Somewhere in between, Grandpa, at sixty, married an eighteen-year-old girl from Apopca, Florida. I thought of Sandra as my grandmother, though as one of the second generation I didn't call her that. It caused a big uproar in the family when Sandra returned to Niagara Falls with him in his motorhome, wearing his Hawaiian shirt. But Grandpa stood his ground and, with an arm around Sandra's slender shoulders, said, "It's easy to kill yourself without dying," or something like that. As for Sandra's family, the rumor was that her mother thought my grandfather was courting her, and so the day that he came to whisk Sandra off to the courthouse was the couple's last encounter with "Mum." Grandpa probably laughed from his deep belly, the one that made him sing great Italian opera, and snatched some oranges on the way out.

What I remember most about Grandpa was when he played the murderer in *Ten Little Indians* and really frightened me with that noose in his hand. I remember eating wonton soup through his three-year wonton-making hobby. I remember his two Cuban stepchildren: Howie and Eddie. (Before Sandra, Grandpa was briefly wedded to a woman from Cuba who could hardly speak English, but was a fantastic cook.) But I remember most of all the young wife whom he left behind, hanging on to the pictures and the overall great feeling he gave her. Now I know it's always hardest for the ones who linger.

That spring after Grandpa died, we cleaned out his little house, and I helped Sandra pack her things for the move back to Florida and back to Mum. While my cousins snatched up the TV, the remaining wontons and pieces of furniture, I took only two items – Grandpa's thesaurus and his King James. Sandra said it was the best possible choice. So I began reading the Bible a lot – everything from the psalms to the gospels. I also began pounding away on Grandpa's beat-up typewriter, thesaurus by my side. With each day, his absence became a little easier, and whenever my spirit got too heavy, I heard him asking, "What's that in your ear?", and with a hearty laugh, I finally understood why Grandpa carried those potatoes on him – even at a wedding, wearing a tuxedo.

See NAGA NAGASHI YO   *S. Guerriri, Buffalo, NY*

❄

DREAM . . .
We had snow: day in, day out, silently it fell in the high Alps, at first dreamless, so deep, so light, as I scaled the terraces to Schatzalp, up and up, and entered nothingness with my

mouth open then waited, hearing my own heart, holding
fast against the icy winds, and stopped to poke the end of
my staff in the snow, to look at the greenish-blue, ice-clear
light emerging from the hole I had made, the flakes so
gentle and without pause, white and whirling, which led
me to slumber and what next? a true awakening deep in
the mountains, glittering like diamonds, where my dream
gave me this word: *For the sake of goodness and love, man shall
let death have no sovereignty over his thoughts.*

                                        H. Castorp, Switzerland

❋

DRIFTING

Some People Think A

Some people think a
blizzard like this
could last
a year

the snow booms
from the north-east
like a drawn-out
organ note

DRIFTING

drift ice	i dream
came into	i return
the fjord	and find
& i cannot	our hut
reach her	under water

in the loneliness of winter imagination
becomes reality in the mind

          if the pack ice
          comes down and
          a bear shows up
          shoot him

but could a storm like
this lift a hut
from the ground
i wonder

          i said, do you hear me
          shoot him in the head

i imagine her there
as the snowdrift passes
over the roof and
stretches to the sea

traps & paraffin   hunting & fishing

       the comet headed
       here (it is bright)
       is my only light

still i cannot find my wife for she is
drifting . . .

      the grave may
      not be its
      goal but that's
      where it's headed

           . . . like the snow,
         too far

i see it is not you yet it is you
but it is so quiet   shhhhh . . .

     shade trees & quiet celebration

(someone who, even in death, has nothing to
do with what is taking place)

     everyday i wait for
     spring when the
     ice will harden
     and i will see her again*

---

*   The search for a lost object is analogous to the quest for the Holy Grail.

```
        will this winter
        be forever
        dark: only in
        my lifetime
```

See COMETS   *A. R. Ammons, N. Carolina*

❈

ELK on our prairie were wiped out during the Massacre Winter we had back in '56. I was born that year so my parents called me Snowdrop. Snowdrop Miller. The other children born alongside me were named Snowflake, Tempest and Storm. There was a Blizzard too: a name that my mother said reminded her of hoof-beats in Virgil's poetry.

She also said the wind rose out of nowhere that day. As the first crystals stirred, there was a rustling sound in the air and millions of pellets approached our farmhouse as an incoming tide. I stood outside waiting for your father, mother said, watching the blizzard rise as puffs of wind tossed white clouds in the air. Flying drifts rushed toward me and covered my ankles, waist and neck. The snow clogged my mouth and nostrils. As if braving a heavy surf, I pushed through the snow toward the house, aiming for the trapdoor that led to the cellar.

On my knees I pushed the snow away until I felt the

outline of an opening. It was impossible to see but, clearing the edges, eventually I found the handle. After a few strong pulls it opened, but the wind made it nearly impossible to get inside. Stepping into the darkness, I let the door fall shut, so the tunnel wouldn't fill with drift, even though it would freeze over soon and I might never escape. The cellar was so dark that I could not even see my hand before my face, but I found the corner and crouched there with an old blanket to wait for your father.

When the cold became stronger than ever, I thought for sure he wouldn't come. We'd all be dead by morning. Dead with the elk,* she said, who froze into ice sculptures on the prairie or trampled each other to death in their scramble for shelter.

See ЖУРÁНИЕ (p. 140)　　　　　　　　**S. Miller, Wisconsin**

❄

* November 9, 1938, also called *Kristallnacht*, was the coldest, darkest day in history: 1500 Jewish shops and 177 synagogues were destroyed and broken glass covered the streets. Joseph Goebbels said, "We will give the Jews a part of the forest, where animals, which are damnably like Jews — the elk, too, has a hooked nose — can mix with them."

EVE,* the time of day that I was lost in a storm as a child, walking, lantern in hand, dispersing the snow with my tiny feet from home; down the steep hill, through the broken hedge, by the stone wall, through the drifts, to the bridge, crossing plank by plank, and then midway disappearing into the bitter wind that puffed up like smoke.

L. Gray, missing

❄

FIBS OF VISION

Svalbard, N of the Arctic Circle, Dec. 10, 1837.
Here the winters are dark and dreary, but at 9 hr 40 m
a dramatic display occurred in the sky as a splendid
aurora borealis stretched from ESE to NW through
the zenith. Two arcs of blinding whiteness appeared
near the horizon beyond the cumulus clouds, and
with a rustling sound, the aurora's rays of light shot
rapidly upward to the zenith and stretched themselves

---

*   EVE is a palindrome. Another example is: *No, it is open on one position*. E is 'the letter of light' and its number is seventy, according to Pythagorean mysticism. Arthur Rimbaud associated vowels with colours, linking E with the colour white and "the glaciers' insolence." Ernst Jünger in *Lob der Vokale* states that E has a "shimmering quality, of vapours and tents."

out, moving from faint green to pale yellow. In restless change they contracted, then broke into many bands of shining silver that cast a reflection like the moon across the ice. The long draperies glided over each other – a glittering garment quivering white. Within moments they melted away, until the faint aurora trembled with its arches, and Capella was seen in the portion beneath, a milky blue-cold covering the entrance to heaven.

See STREAMERS   *R. Snow, Svalbard*

❅

FORGETFUL, careless, dreamy, free like childhood, when winter sheets the earth in white. When the archduke takes us out in a sled one afternoon, and we are surrounded by snow in the mountains, afraid.

T. S. Eliot, New England

❅

FRIGID. When Mama was really messed up she carried around a doll all the time. On rare occasions she placed it in a wicker baby carriage – the flexible kind with the handles. Then she'd reach under the recliner for her knitting needles to make the doll baby a seaweed-colored sweater with matching cap. The doll had one lazy green eye, and one not-so-lazy brown eye, so when Mama thrust it in my face, I turned my head away. She upended its porcelain body — not to punish it but to punish me. *Wahhhhh,* the baby cried with plangent ewe-like resonance. I grimaced. Some day, I thought, the dolly will pull a Pinocchio and come after me à la razor-sharp instrument with the intention of gouging out my black eyes. Maybe he would even use Mama's knitting needles to make the job easy-peasy. But I vowed to fight him the whole way. Or her. Whichever. Pinocchio-like Doll = Familial Discomfort.

And you slept with him. I know you did. You say you didn't, but you damn well did. Brian came to my rescue when I was sixteen, sexually unfrequented and tired of everything: tired of my Mama Josie's affairs, tired of Papa Noah's impotence, tired of older sister Martha ditching us for her Motley Crue-style boyfriend, tired of brother Jonah crapping in bank drive-thru vessels out of nighttime boredom. I couldn't control the quadruplets any longer. I couldn't force happiness, coerce them into loving each other, or will them to love me by clicking my heels and chanting, *There's no place like home; there's no place like home.* Could I? God had rolled the dice and I got double ones. No wonder they called life a crap shoot.

When I first met Brian, Mama and I were visiting at his parents' house. (Every so often Mama would hustle me over there – down the street and around the corner – because she was trying to make nicey with the neighbors.) But during this particular visit, the robust and sandy-haired Brian appeared out of nowhere, gamboling down the stairway with a grin. I wondered where he got his height. Both of his parents were dwarfish. Soon, this was the scene: Brian reclining in his family's rocking chair; Mama a.k.a. Josie crouching next to it; and me sunk awkwardly into a huge divan. Meanwhile, Brian's mother made us cappuccinos in the kitchen. The hissing of the milk steamer sounded like a weeping willow capturing the breeze in its swaying leaves.

"Oh, Brian, we're so glad you're back here from Indiana," Mama cooed. "Aren't you, Libby? We've heard so much about you."

I nodded, token-like, and Brian beamed.

Mama's crouching made her butt look huge; it jutted out and said, "Helloooo! Look at me!" as her billowing boobs rested on her thighs. Her black eyes were like a Siamese cat's when she looked at Brian.

We are Siamese if you please. We are Siamese if you don't please.

"I got laid off at my job in Cleveland," Brian said. "So I moved back home for awhile. No sweat! I should get another job right away with all my skill."

"Oh, really? What do you do?"

"At Durez I did . . . uh," he cleared his throat. "Ya know, assembly line stuff."

"Oh! How neat!" Mama exclaimed.

I looked around but said nothing. The various flower and ivy patterns scattered about the room on wallpapers and fabrics dizzied me; and for a minute I swore I was inside a greenhouse looking for the exit because the stench of old plants was making me sneeze and wheeze. *Ahhhchoooo!*

"But I can sell too," Brian said.

"Really? Me too! What have you sold?" Mama asked.

"Ya know, the usual. Rainbow vacuums an' stuff."

Brian. Brain. Coincidence? Oh, definitely.

"What a great experience! How old are you?" Mama looked over at me and winked.

"I'm twenty, ma'am."

He's twenty? Why did I wear my red hair in pigtails? I looked *sooo* Pippi Longstocking.

"Thank you," I said as Brian's mom set our mugs of cappuccino on the coffee table.

"Fab!" Mama nestled into the plush chartreuse carpet, legs broadcast in front of her — and the boobs still billowed. *Josie and the Pussycats.*

I rolled my eyes, then carefully put my own mug to my lips and slowly sipped. The liquid hit my tongue, it seared and scraped all the way down and left the roof of my mouth like sandpaper. My taste buds had temporarily gone to pot.

"Mmm . . ." Mama remarked as she embarked on her first sip — and as I watched the dark fluid pour into her mouth I was suddenly glad we had come to this place for sweet conversation and scalded coffee; and when Mama's panic-stricken face revealed her torment I relaxed. She bolted into the kitchen.

"We just bought the machine, actually," Brian's mother said.

Brian turned toward me and away from Mama. "So, Libby, what do you do?"

"High school, mostly."

"She's an artist," Mama piped in as she returned from the kitchen with squirrel mouth.

"Cool!" Brian exclaimed.

I nodded. "I like figurative art."

The art conversation ended there. The amount of cultural awareness invading the room was equal to the amount of love, which was in the negative digits according to my gauge. I looked at Mama and silently conveyed to her, with widened eyes, that I was ready to leave.

When we stood near the doorway and I pulled on my down coat, woollen scarf and mittens, Brian asked, "Want to go to a movie sometime?"

When he spoke, his chin, so carefully cut, looked mechanical. When he laughed his eyes lit the room pale green; and when he stood next to me – 5′11″ next to my 5′8″ – his full lips were just above mine. I never stood so close to a man before; and when I smelled his aftershave, I tingled.

"Do you like Jackie Chan?"

I did not particularly like Jackie Chan. But there were two

kinds of guy in Buffalo: those who digged cars and those who didn't. Those who didn't dig cars had a fetish for sports. Seldom did they go to the cinema.

So nearly prostrating myself in the hopes of having a movie-going companion, and a cute one at that, I said, "Yes! I love Jackie! Do you?"

He nodded. I smiled. And we said goodbye.

Mama and I drove toward home. She cranked up the radio, playing bad 70s disco, so we wouldn't have to speak. She jiggled in her seat to "Hooked on a Feeling," as I watched my breath make visible puffs in the bitter air of the car. Mama's little two-door would take ten minutes to warm up, but by that time we'd be home. I wrote my name in the frost on the window with my index finger then wiped it away, exposing a vista of falling snow outside. We passed each of our neighbors' houses lit up like primary-colored cupcakes for the holiday season. They entranced me. I looked inside house after house where friends gathered, chatting as they looked out at the wintry scene. Scattered about the warm rooms – on a stool, bench or windowsill – lay the gifts of the evening. One house had an elaborate Nativity scene in the front yard. Everything was there: Joseph and Mary, Christ and the manger, the hay, the Three Wise Men, the Immaculate Conception . . . a lone star. I caught the Virgin's intense stare, and I thought she might tell me something, but the light turned green and Mama drove on. The empty branches of the trees poked up at the sky, which boasted an ominous gray cloud, the one that stretched for miles and lingered for months over upstate New York; the gray cloud that we all knew could be credited to factories and landfills. After this, I thought, the long winter departs, spring comes, then summer. As we pulled into our driveway several minutes later, Mama asked rhetorically, "Isn't Brian the cutest?"

Well, he certainly was a fast-mover. A week later he opened his guitar case and revealed his instrument to me, an electric guitar on which he could play "Stairway to Heaven;" then another week later he unveiled his *other* instrument (both to which I was virgin). *What the heck is that? Look, but don't touch!*

He took me cruising in his car, a royal blue, two-door, manual-speed Pontiac Sunbird; and with Def Leppard or Rush guiding us along the Scajaqueda highway, I heard the wind off the river providing background vocals. We talked sometimes, but mostly savored the silence or the music between us. I envied the Hawaiian hula girl plastered to the dashboard as she dipped and bobbed. She was 99 percent love and 1 percent magic. With long dark hair and a grass green skirt, her breasts as ripe as mangoes, she was so unlike me. I had fiery red hair, mosquito-bite-sized boobs, and baby fat everywhere else. I couldn't gyrate either, with hands that trembled whenever he touched me, and a tongue that either flipped around too much or didn't move at all because his face was so close . . . so close. *Look at me now.*

On a snowy day in January, he picked me up from my waitressing job at Perkin's. I spotted him outside the glass doors with his motor running. And running, I flew out the door and stepped into the night. I watched Brian drum his right fingers on the upper rim of the steering wheel. His left hand weeded through his sandy blond hair, which flopped back in his eyes. Motor Running = First Tinge of Doubt. *Uh oh, my soul mate is supposed to be frugal. It's written in the stars.* Still, I forged ahead, seeing what he had in store for me. I opened the door and slid in; the smell of maple syrup on my apron mingled with his Cool Water cologne. Then, finally, on the corner of Delaware Ave and Sheridan, at a red light, he leaned in and kissed me. Bang! Lightning streaked up the sky and ploughed my heart and I thought oh!

Oh!

"Pull over, Brian. I'm going to be sick!"

"What?" With an abrupt movement we were on the side of the road, hazard lights blinking.

"Ya okay?"

"Yes. Just don't look," I said, then opened the door and eased out of the car. I threw up — there and then. Pulled over, door open, on the side of Sheridan Drive, on the pristine white lawn of the Talking Pages, on cue. The sausage links

I'd snatched from the $1.99 breakfast platter were now chunked and green and nestled in the snow like worms. Five-hundred thirty-nine calories jettisoned. It wasn't so hard. *Everything was too perfect for words.*

When I entered our two-story house in Buffalo, the smell of yellow American cheese floated from the kitchen into the hallway, which usually smelled like old garbage. Papa was making late-night tuna melts. I removed my down coat and adjusted my brown polyester skirt with matching, vertically striped blouse before I stepped into the kitchen.

"Hello, Papa," I greeted.

"Oh hi, Lib. I was just trying a new edition of my famous—" he answered with a low mumble, but before he could continue, I swam away from his voice, away from shore in a fight against the ocean current and, hands on my proverbial ears, into the bathroom.

With the door closed, I checked to see if lipstick had been smeared on my chin. A little red splotch appeared below my bottom lip. I smoothed my long, thin hair away from my forehead with a splash of water and then scrubbed away at the unwanted patch of chin irritation until it was raw. I rinsed my rank-tasting mouth with Listerine, but the flavor wouldn't go away. The aftertaste of vomit was all I had to remember of Brian's first kiss. And then my hearing returned and Papa's one-sentence, three-minute-mumble so far was quite like a bee's nest that had exploded outside the door and would invade my privacy any minute now. *Stop! Just stop!*

Papa's métier was breadcrumbs. He made his calls in the morning from the kitchen bar, discussing consistency, as the serpentine coils of the cord would go *swish, swish* like broom whiskers on someone's backside.

He only liked me because I looked like you, bitch. Someone asked me at what age I realized I was beautiful and I replied, "I don't know." But I do know; I never realized it, especially not then. I still don't realize it. Because I am a precise replica of Mama – a plastic blow-up doll – complete with her dark Jezebel eyes and childbearing hips. Mama's beauty is a façade, something intangible; the glance of a gypsy and the rock of a whore cause a reaction in any male, fooled into believing they see beauty like a bull is drawn to anything red, but it is only a trick, an illusion. I am an illusion.

Brian kissed me again and again. He stopped by on weekend nights and we hung out. We talked about hockey or bowling, whatever he wanted to talk about, in the living room, alone for a brief moment until Mama came home from work and joined us, when I'd say with faux surprise, *Hey! There's Mama Jo! Hi Mama!*
    "Want to play pinochle?" Brian asked me.
I hated pinochle, so I looked around the room for an out:

an empty crossword puzzle, a dirty dish, scraps on the floor, even companionship. Jonah was home for once, but in the basement dressed up as a monster and into a heavy-duty role-playing game with his pals. Martha was on her non-visitation streak after moving out with her boyfriend the previous year. And Papa, as usual, sat in his recliner with a book resting on his knee and hunched over it – a vulture over its prey. Every five minutes Papa mumbled but no one gave him answers.

Nothing doing.

"Pinochle? Sure, I guess so," I said.

"Cool!" Brian said.

Mama Josie was the pinochle queen, so there we were, the three of us at the walnut dining-room table, cards sliding over the leaf edges back-n-forth with a *shwooo, shwooo*. The jack of hearts stared back at me and I had to get up, dizzy. I made a batch of instant brownies. After letting them cool, I placed five on a plate and set it on the table between Mama and Brian. After Brian took his, I went for the one with the least nuts. As my hand wrapped around the moist edges of the chocolate square, Mama belted out, "That's the one I want! Don't take the one I want!"

The Alaskan wolf prints on the dining-room walls shook with disbelief.

I pulled away from the brownie and glanced at Brian, who was intently scrutinizing his pinochle hand.

"Okay, Mama. Sorry." Then I reached for the other one,

which was equally nice. They both had the same amount of calories, nearly a thousand, and mine would just get flushed eventually anyhow. *Life is all addiction and subtraction.*

I'd made it all the way to 11th Grade without making more than two friends, but suddenly kids began to notice me. Guys who never spoke to me before leaned on my locker in their flannel shirts and ripped jeans and said, "Lookin' good! Did you change your hair?" Female acquaintances, some-times cheerleaders, said, "Wow, you've lost some weight. You look great!" During lunch I picked at: 1 Celery Stick, 3 Saltine Crackers, ¼ Container of Non-fat, Non-flavored Yogurt. I watched the hoard of them eat way-too-much-cheese pizza, loaded-with-fat fried chicken and pack-on-the-pounds chocolate cake and thought, *Look at them all. They're out of control!*

Brian wanted to have sex, of course. After everyone had gone to bed, we sat alone on the sofa. He slung his arm around my shoulders and slurped my ear. I slithered in delight.

He whispered, "You're so sexy."

"Mmmm . . ." I smiled in the dark and kissed his neck at his Adam's apple.

He moved his warm hands up my shirt and squeezed my breasts. "Can I come upstairs?" he asked.

"No, you'd better not," I said, resting my hand on his blue

jeans. I didn't know where to place it, but he covered my hand with his and guided me to the right place.

"Honey! Why?" Sweat trickled from his sideburns.

"My parents!"

"Don't you want it? I know you want it!"

"I want it, but you know I can't. We have to wait."

I pushed his hands away, adjusted my T-shirt and ran upstairs. I heard the door shut too loudly for midnight and the engine of his Sunbird roar out of the driveway. I was angry at myself for being so prudishly callow and for caring too much. I was angry at Mama for being the kind of woman who wouldn't have pushed a man like Brian away.

Mama always told me Papa was impotent, she told me even before I knew what that word meant.

The following week Brian went away to visit friends in Cleveland, three hours from Buffalo. He sent me a postcard that said, "No fun without you. Be home soon. Love, Bri." True, not eloquent prose, but his script was calligraphic. I'd never known anyone who cared enough or was patient enough to practice their handwriting with a fountain pen, over and over, until it was almost Medieval. I missed the ten-minute rides home from the restaurant when I could be silent in the aftermath of rude customers and Brian wouldn't mind. So while he was away, I inhaled in a matter of hours: 1 Carton of Ben & Jerry's Chubby Hubby ½ Bag of Ridged Potato Chips 6 Chocolate Chip Cookies 1 Big Mac 1 Large Order of Fries Takeout Moo Goo Gai Pan 1 Bag of Licorice 2 Almond Joy Bars. Purging was an easy procedure – lifting up the toilet seat and gagging at the stench of dried-up urine, kneeling one knee up, one knee down on the hard tiles, gripping the sink with my left hand and then sticking my right index finger as far down my throat as possible, leaning over the open bowl, jabbing sometimes once, sometimes thrice, whatever would make all that sick hilarity come up from my stomach and burn my esophagus . . . Exhilarating!

Mama's uncles had "touched her," she told me, when she was young. Those same uncles had touched me too, and all the other girls in our family, but the majority of us had turned out all right. Take my cousin Esther, for example. She had a good marriage, two lovely daughters, and played the organ like a dream! So I didn't think molestation provided an excuse for Mama to run off and get married young, have three children, nurse 'em, and then, after forty, sleep with everyone but your husband and neglect your three children. In the old days Mama threw her head back and smiled; she held Papa's hand like a little girl; she planted kisses on our ginger hair. Sunday was family night, when the three of us girls would make pizza dough and laugh, kicking up the dusty flour with our slippers. Then we'd all eat pizza on paper plates and wipe our chins with paper towels while watching Disney movies; and I thought, we're truly happy. Now Mama was away on Sundays flirting with every wang-toting thing while Papa and me sat wallowing with empty spaces in our hearts that we believed nobody else could fill.

Did you covet them too, Mama? When Brian returned from Ohio, he carried two life-sized bears, one under each arm, and gave them to me.

"How did you know I liked bears?" I asked Brian, and after he left, I tossed the hard pieces of plastic-haired junk to the back of my closet. People always say, "It's the thought that counts," but for me, if the thought isn't motivated by understanding, it really doesn't count at all. Flowers came too (sunflowers picked up at grocery store), and then jewelry – always, always before pinochle. He told me on a Tuesday driving home from work that he really liked me, that he loved me in fact; and we locked tongues, turning toward one another in his Sunbird so my pelvis pushed into the gearshift, nearly breaking.

I slept in the attic-turned-bedroom on a futon underneath a skylight, where I gazed up at a backdrop of sky behind wooden telephone poles and their hundreds of connecting wires. I dozed off on my stomach and when I awoke during the night, I remembered that statistically 96 percent of women who sleep on their stomachs are in love. For me, this was clearly not the case. I just liked the feeling of my belly squashed against the hard wood of a futon frame, which had an optimum emptiness effect with only a thin layer of mattress in between. Hollow Cavern Facing Down = Feeling of Greater Emptiness.

One afternoon Brian and I stretched out on our backs in the front yard, fanning our limbs until our two bodies and our arc-like movements made celestial impressions in the pure snow; and for a moment the sun made a brief appearance from behind the gray cloud.

"You're too skinny, Lib. You could use some pounds," Brian said several weeks later, his right ankle propped on his other knee as we sat side-by-side on the couch. "I completely understand . . . Sometimes I'm not in the mood to eat either."

He handed me two books. One was a health book on female issues some moms never discuss when growing up. It was fittingly titled: *What Some Moms Never Tell You When You Are Growing Up*. Well, I didn't think I'd get much out of the book. The other book I received was entitled, *Dealing With Co-Dependency Issues*.

He patted my knee and it made a hollow knocking sound. "You have such bony knees! Just like Papa Noah!" I smiled weakly.

"Okay, well goodbye, sweetie, take care," Brian said, still

staring. I remained quiet in my seat with my hands acting as a cushion for my ass to ease the pain.

He rose from the divan and pivoted on his heels. "I'm ready for that pinochle match, Jo!" he shouted, dashing out the door, while I remained watching the pendulum rock of the grandfather clock; and the weeks that followed passed quickly, all those other days when the only words I heard were: "How are you feeling today? What did you do today? Did you eat?" Those questions from Brian, from Mama Jo, from Papa Noah comprised the trinity that my holy ones handed me, the three strands always in sequence and always clustered together like one being. But I didn't reply. Instead, I thought of the Nativity. Everything rots away, little by little. I had enough brains to recognize it.

Come springtime and after the first big melt I began to see the grass again. At the end of my work-shift I punched the time clock, walked out and wished for the strength to keep going and never return to that late-night, truck-stop diner where people shouted at me; "Hey, where's that ketchup for my burger, lady?," "What is this crap?" and "Get me a coffee, will ya?"

Brian's car became a haven.

But tonight, without hello, he roared, "What is going on? You're not having any periods?"

I shrank. "How do you know?"

"Josie told me, Lib."

"It's none of your business," I said.

"Yes it is! I'm your boyfriend." He put his hand on my leg. I swiped his hand away. "Brian, I can't be in a relationship right now. I'm not ready."

"Don't avoid the subject. Why is this happening?"

"Why is what happening?" The hula girl on the dashboard shook her hips.

"You've changed."

"Whatever." *I haven't changed*, I thought, *you just never knew me.*

When we got to my house he followed me inside; squeezed through the door just before I closed it in his face; stepped on my heels as I ascended the stairs into the kitchen; grabbed my elbow as I rounded the corner.

"Wait, Lib. We can work this out."

"Just go away," I said, lowering my head. *I don't need you.*

"Okay, fine," he said with a turn; and his ears turned cherry-colored as if he heard my thoughts. I made my way upstairs to my bedroom and listened for the door to slam shut. The house was quiet for five minutes and then I heard him downstairs in the kitchen talking in whispered tones to Mama. I sensed she was making him a strawberry daiquiri. Whispering + Daiquiris = Bliss. *Damn her.*

Psychologists, talk-show hosts and magazines (e.g. John Gray, Oprah, *Maxim*, *Cosmopolitan*) generally agree on the top ten things a husband should never say to his spouse to guarantee a good, solid marriage. They are:

1. You look beautiful, today.
2. You look tired.
3. Are you going to wear that?
4. Are you going to eat that?
5. Don't get weird on me.
6. You're evil.
7. I'm working late tonight.
8. How much did you spend?
9. What did YOU do all day?
10. She (any female other than your wife, including pets) is attractive.

Papa had never, in twenty-five years of marriage, said any of these things to Mama. So what was the problem? Could Ruth Westheimer be wrong?

"I got Brian a job at my company," Mama told me the next morning as she bit into her cinnamon toast.

"Why?" I asked.

"Because he's a good salesman."

"Oh, is he?" I said, then took the stairs two at a time for a fast exit. I walked two miles to school with my hands in my pockets, and could feel my legs because of the holes in the liner. My toes, like frozen blocks of ice, hit up against the front of my boots, even though most of the snow had melted and the air felt warmer. I couldn't wait to get to art class, where I could emancipate myself in a self-portrait, *Girl with A Pearl Earring.* For weeks I stroked and stroked until my Old Holland oils captured her unpretentious virginal gaze. Alas, I was staring at myself in the form of a tiny Dutch girl. Then, one day, my trusty Isabey Special Hog-Hair Bristle # 6 Filbert brush slipped out of my hand and clattered on the floor. Flesh Ochre rubbed across the tiles. "Oops," I said, looking up. Then to the onlookers, fellow painters, an explanation: "How stupid of me. I don't know what happened. One minute I had it, and the next it just slipped out of my hand . . . "

The day after I finished final exams, right before summer vacation, Mama and Papa checked me in to the mental hospital so specialists could pump food into me through clear plastic tubes. They said they couldn't handle me anymore. I was refusing to eat.

"Something must be done!" Mama exclaimed.

The first week the nurses wheeled me in a pushchair up and down the dismal hallways, up-n-down, back-n-forth, in a bipolar motion that was somehow comforting. "You're too fragile to walk," the nurses said, but I was fine, and remembered the words of my idol Tess: "Now punish me . . . Whip me, crush me; you need not mind those people under the rick, I shall not cry out. Once victim, always victim." The corridors of the hospital smelled like ammonia, with hints of cigarette smoke and alcohol that dawdled on everyone's breath. At times the others spoke to me in mellow tones, with tics, telling me their histories. I listened politely, but it was all a crock: the rape, violence, addiction, religious fanaticism, obsession. Returning to my room, I forgot them all.

Everyday at 6 a.m., the nurses weighed me. They told me I was 80 pounds, and I thought, *oh gawd*. Like the other girls, I drank loads of water before my weigh-in to appear to have gained. If they believed I'd gained, I could have visitors. And avoid the group confessional sessions.

I painted every day. My psychotherapist, Dr. Wilinski, called it that magic word: *therapy*. The results hung all over my walls: bewitching, Boticelliesque, bare women who drew me into their sadness – pursed lips, downcast eyes and tangled hair, in some instances pulled back to reveal the whiteness of their necks. One nude in particular, the darkest queen of them all, and plumpest – full breasts with round pink nipples, arching hips, rolling thighs and a fleshy paunch – resembled me. Frailty was in her eyes and their stark white eyelids without lashes, setting off a muddy gaze.

The nurses continued feeding me; and finally I was ready for visitors. Papa came alone on family day and cradled my skin-n-bones, transparent hand in his while mumbling to me with his chin wobbling and his glasses sliding slowly down his Hungarian nose. Mama Jo and Brian visited me together. Like two old chums they carried each other's things, chatted about work issues when I was quiet and exchanged furtive glances. Brian brought me gifts and Mama looked on with smiles. I thought, *No. It couldn't be. She wouldn't.*

Mama said, when my ex-boyfriend left the room to fetch some water, "Say something! He still really likes you. Don't you like him?"

"No. I hate him."

But I liked the sheets he brought me.

After I'd gained 10 pounds, my handsome psychotherapist Dr. Wilinski — forty-something, short greying hair, metal-rimmed glasses, a large round nose and intense blue eyes — told me I could leave the hospital if I reached 100 pounds. *Fat chance*, I thought. He asked if he could interview me for his documentary and I agreed, if only for the perks: a moment to be near him, to hear him speak with his gentle Polish accent, to wade in his bookish aura. Stripped down to my cotton flowery underwear, I sat in a straight-back metal chair in front of the camera as he focused. I crossed my hands in front of my breasts.

"Just relax," Dr. Wilinski told me as his lithe body led by gazelle-like legs walked around the camera. I admired his hips as he adjusted the controls. He sat down behind the camera so I could see his hands settling on his crossed leg and his black suede shoes. Then the camera whirred and I was face-to-face with my alter ego.

"How do you feel about your body?" Dr. Wilinski asked. I looked down and then back up again. "I hate it. I need to lose weight."

"What part of your body do you hate the most?"

"My stomach."

"Why?"

I thought the answer was obvious, but I answered anyway. "It's huge. I feel pregnant."

"But you're not pregnant."

"No . . ." *Dr. Wilinski, I'm a virgin.*

"So it is a sexual feeling?"

I hesitated and shuffled my bare feet on the tiles. Handsome Psychologist + Sexual Discussion = Blushing. "Um . . . no . . ."

"Try to explain it, Libby. *Put it into words.*"

"It's like I have something growing inside me that doesn't belong there."

Dr. Wilinski cleared his throat. Then, he asked, "Does sex frighten you, Libby?"

I bit my bottom lip. "Well, no. What happens afterward frightens me."

He lowered his voice. "What is that? What happens afterward?"

"You know," I said, shrinking.

He tapped his fingers on his knee, waiting for a reply.

"Abandonment, Dr. Wilinski."

He uncrossed his leg. "Let's talk about Abandonment." I wanted to tell him about Mama, Brian, Papa, my uncles and breadcrumbs. I wanted to divulge my great fear that every person whom I loved would walk out on me. I had a premonition: I *knew* they would leave. But I couldn't tell the good doctor.

"Tell me why you think you are fat, then," he said.

"Because I'm just like my mother. I *am* my mother. But I don't want to be . . . I *hate* her." I surprised myself with my honesty.

"And so you starve yourself to avoid her? For revenge maybe?"

"Mmmhmm." The interview was turning into the usual psychotherapy session. I could almost predict what he'd say next and what would be a good response.

"Isn't there another way? I mean, isn't she then controlling you because everything you do and think revolves around not becoming her?"

"Probably."

"What are you thinking right now?" he asked.

"I'm trying not to think because when I do my thoughts follow me around and eventually, I run into myself again – it's disgusting."

"Okay, what do you feel right now?"

This was easy. "Power, control."

"That's what you want to feel . . ." he began.

I nearly forgot the camera was there and removed my hands from my breasts. "I guess so. You're right. I'm in chains." I smiled to myself – doing pretty well.

The good doctor stirred, and perhaps he was zooming in, so I looked away, at the ceiling, and zoned in on a dead mosquito.

"What do *you* see?" I asked him.

He turned off the camera.

"Thank you for participating," he said.

That's right. I'm just a guinea pig. A lab rat.

Three months is definitely too long to wait for someone to get healthy, especially if their sanity is in question, so I didn't blame Brian when he stopped coming to visit me. And by the time I got better and was discharged, 15 pounds heavier, he'd moved back to Cleveland. It was time to commence my senior year at Kenmore High. But now that Mama had lost her job to "downsizing," she had nowhere to go and nothing to do. Hence, Mama's doll obsession sprang from loneliness, not the kind that you feel when your daughter gets married or your dog passes away, the kind of loneliness that you feel if your lover leaves you. Mama cradled the doll for five months at every chance, amidst the long hours lying on our country-rose carpet, legs up, head reeling under the power of Sony headphones – every day, without speech. Every day, in the same place as we stepped around her to get to the stairway; every day

I practiced ignorance and every day whispered to myself, "Don't mind her."

Eventually Mama took off, moved to Florida, without giving the rest of us notice. No note – suicide or otherwise – no e-mail, voicemail or snail mail. Just the constant ticking of the upright clock and a sizeable oil stain in the driveway where her Toyota used to sit. The first week we waited for her to return as hastily as she departed, but she didn't. The second week I cleaned the house, taking special care of the living-room rug, in case she wanted to return to lying on the floor. I even set her headphones out. But by the third week, when we hadn't heard from her, I said to Papa, "She's not coming back." The fourth passed, then the fifth, so I tucked away all her sweatshirts and cowboy hats in drawers and closets. I moved "family" items like photographs, postcards and lamps to places where they looked *so much better*. I wadded the decks of cards down the kitchen drain and blasted them with the hi-power spray water gun that we usually used to rinse pasta. The rooms of the house where I grew up smelled like fresh pine scent instead of mothballs. I painted, healed, recreated Libby. I touched the piano again, and refurnished the room with Chopin. I fell in love with love as I sang along with Mimi in *La Bohème*. This way, I could not hear Papa mumble. "She's coming back," he said, "Don't worry . . ."

Five months later and the first winter post-Brian, Mama

finally rang from Florida. She spoke to Papa first. "When are you coming home, honey?" he asked, over and over. "Yes, hmm . . . Yes," he nodded, over and over. "Your car broke down? Oh, I'm sorry to hear that. Well, we miss you." I watched my Papa, phone near his ear, turn rapidly into mush like fresh boiled potatoes in the Cuisinart. I knew he believed every damn lie she told him. I knew he believed she was coming back. I knew she wasn't coming back. He handed the phone to me.

From her cheap motel, Mama greeted, "Hi, Libby sweetie!" and I sensed it was cheap because the cockroaches scampered along the floorboards loud enough for me to hear.

"It's Mama Jo!" she added.

Of course it is.

"Hi," I said, trying to hide my surprise or lack of surprise.

"Are you taking care of Papa?"

"Of course."

"Great!" she said, breathing heavily.

"Mama, are you . . . uh . . . okay?"

She smacked her lips. "Oh, yes, I've just needed some away-time. You know how it is, don't you Libby, you understand . . ."

"Do you have a job?"

"I'm collecting seashells, making necklaces and selling them at craft shows . . . And I've found the most wonder-

ful doctor and he says I have manic depression. He wants
me to go on Lithium!"

Lithium? Don't they make something stronger?

"That may be a good idea," I said.

"So, Libby – did you know why Brian and I kept talking
after you broke up?"

"No I don't, Mama." The handset rested between my
shoulder and earlobe.

"It was because we were always talking about YOU. We
wanted to help YOU, Lib." I heard the sound of a seagull in
the background. She must have stepped outside.

"Oh," I said, and I knew that the wall would not come
down between us, not for a long time.

"Brian and I had a connection, a common bond," she
explained through orange juice-stained teeth. "We came
together in a common interest like Papa and I never did.
I just don't want you to be mad at me. I really care for him.
He's a good guy."

Connection with Brian + Papa's Impotence =

"Did you sleep with him?"

She paused. "No, sweetie. Our relationship was emotional, not sexual. Don't be mad. It didn't have anything to
do with you."

*Of course it didn't. Nothing has to do with me. I am exempt from
all dictionaries and encyclopaedias. I am the absence of meaning.*

"I'm not mad," I said. "But I don't believe you . . . " and
so, for the first time I was honest with her – a short but

candid moment as I imagined her in a pair of faded jeans and a sweatshirt that took the chill out of a winter Florida morning. The day would turn warm, I knew, when she'd toss off her clothes to reveal a bathing suit from which her flesh, dark like figs, would spill. Later she'd sip a strawberry daiquiri poolside while her ill-starred family was stuck north in some snow bank. Got to hand it to her, though. Buffalo winters, Florida was the place to go.

See ANGEL   **L. Ferguson, Manhattan**

※

There was a **GALE** so fierce that sparrows resting on the window ledges of the Sun building could not fly against it. Every few minutes they started out to stand still, wings fluttering in vain, or attempted to fly with the winds but were hustled along like stones thrown with great force.* I spied from below, clinging to a lamppost, trying to withstand the gale's enormous pressure; and watching the sparrows, learned to *submit to the power of air*, which took my legs, my arms and carried me away, into the sleet which struck my face, so my moustache froze, my eyebrows too, and little icicles formed on my eyelashes.

See TRUTH   ***A gentleman who lived on 128th Street,***
New York

---

* Virgil compared the ghosts of the dead to thronging birds.

GAY.
> Deck the halls with boughs of holly,
> Fa-la-la-la-la,
>   la-la-la-la.
> 'Tis the season to be jolly,
> Fa-la-la-la-la,
>   la-la-la-la.
> Don we now our . . .
> > *The Ramblin' Lou Family Singers, Ontario*

❄

HAIL, Orbs of Ice, encircling one another, some white, some opaque, some near an Inch in Diameter. I first encounter'd these great stones in *Gresham College*, London, on the morning of May 18, 1680, shortly after I awoke, at 10¾ Hour. I observed these Particulars. The Fore-part of the Night it rained continuously and at three or Four o' the Clock, I was jostled from my sleep by a violent shower on my window and thunder and lightning. If any Hail fell then, I know not, being in Bed, but it continued to rain and thunder much, 'til about Nine, when the sky clear'd and the Sun shone brightly. At Ten o' the Clock the Clouds began to thicken and the sky grew very dark, and it thunder'd very near. There was a great noise out of the Sky like shooting pebbles.

Soon there began to fall Hailstones, some as large as pistol bullets, others as big as chicken eggs. The smallest ones were round and white, like chalk, or sugarplums. From the manner of their figure, I believe that the small White Globule in the middle, the size of a pea, was the first drop that concreted into Hail; and, in falling through the clouds, congealed the Water into Orbs.

Dr Hooke, London

❄

HARMONY – n. *Agreement between two; combination of simultaneous notes to form chords; sweet or melodious sound; collation of parallel narratives.**

December 10

Dear Butterfly—

You must one day review our correspondence, which began exactly a year ago today. (See attached: I've enclosed a short sampling of some of my personal favourites.) Thus far, our exchange already abolishes any truth that might have been contained in your phrase of this morning's phone call, when you said your novel is about "a relationship even shorter than ours was . . ." True, we only had each other for

---

* "True symbolism depends on the fact that things, which may differ from one another in time, space, material, nature, and many other limitative characteristics, can possess and exhibit the same essential quality." – Titus Burkhardt.

seven months, but you are staring at a handful of pebbles in a mosaic of vast complexity. Step away from the wall and you will see a narrative that swirls. The moments of passion, rage and rejection, the muted anguish of feigned indifference, the precious pools of shared rapport are all notes of a symphony in which you and I are the principal players. It began, as you wrote in a postcard, when you were "born" loving me. I do not know where the notes may lead us. There are other themes in the score that we both have to explore. But please never speak of us in the past tense.

There are implications for art in that rather vehement rejection of the *particular* in favour of the *universal*. One revolves around the notion of a hologram's three-dimensional representation of an object or a scene. We have talked before of the almost magical fact that if you take the hologram's plate, roughly analogous to the negative of a photograph, break it up into small pieces and shine a laser through one of the fragments, the whole scene reappears. The totality is contained within the part.

On the other hand, if you cut a photographic negative into pieces and shine a light through it, the only thing recreated is the fragment of the image captured on the small part of the negative. Great art is holographic, containing the universal within its particularity. Most art is photographic, mistaking the fragment for the whole. But most art mistakes itself for the universal when it is momentary. Achieving universality in any art form that eliminates 2 or 3 or 4 of the senses is a daunting challenge. To approach the artist's task wearing intellectual and aesthetic blinders of assuming the fragment is the whole seems a needless hindrance to shoulder. When you, perhaps unintentionally, imply the end of our relationship you mistake the present fragment for the universal. We are not done. We are far from over – as artists, people, or lovers.

Moth

P.S. Are you still in Russia?

December 24

Dear Moth,

Be careful. I understand that some one is sending postcards of polar bears from the World Wildlife Federation with the intention of enticing naïve schoolboys. These polar bear images cause the recipient to develop an uncontrollable urge to spend a wild night with the sender of the card. You know how those uncontrollable urges are: first, the sender of the card calls the recipient on the phone, then hangs up, scrubs her body with dead-sea salts until her skin is smooth, rinses and dries and streaks across the floor to open the door. She puts a lantern on the stairs in the snow and goes back inside. The recipient, waiting outside, sees the flickering light and gets out of his car. He proceeds to the front door, which he finds unlocked, and enters, stamping his feet. The sender suddenly reveals herself from behind the curtain. Then she slowly undresses him in the darkness, peeling off layer after

layer, then spends the evening making love to him – careful not to wake her son sleeping upstairs.
Butterfly

December 25
Dear Butterfly—

OK, I left – what, a half-hour ago? – and am still completely without a bone in my body. It had been a while since I'd been so completely de-boned. That's an interesting question, oh my questioning lover: what is it that makes a day like today unique? I get de-boned and you wear the number "oo" – why? Or why wonder? Thank you for seeing me. I would love to rendezvous again on Sunday for a couple of hours from say – oh, 11:15 until 1:15. Would you check your calendar and see if that would be possible?
Moth

Dear B—

I was just joking about Bob Dylan. I don't hate him. I don't love him, and I'm really not keen on his image, but his verses are lovely. Really.
Moth

January 17
Dear Moth,
As I embark on my first novel my thoughts float around the current disfavor in which the "coming of age" work finds

61

itself. I wonder if that might be the result of the way the works are executed, as opposed to a flaw in the form. To "come of age" implies a movement into something better than that which preceded it. Do you think an unintended arrogance might permeate most examples of the genre?
Butterfly

Hmmm, B—

I see your novel as the presentation of alternate realities that have occurred in your characters' lives.

Moth

Feb 27

Dear M,

You and I are like ice and fire. The ice is best when illuminated by flames, and the fire is most beautiful reflected in the lens of the ice. But when drawn together the flames melt the ice creating water that, in turn, drowns the flames. Out of mutual beauty grows mutual destruction — never intentional, never planned, but inevitable. Why can't the clock ever run backwards, why can't that wild craziness last? Why do we have to grow up? Wouldn't it be nicer with just you and me and Tigger and Pooh as the sun set gently over the Hundred-acre Wood? Why do you have to be so damn arrogant?
Butterfly

March 1

Butterfly—

Ice vs. fire; free choice vs. necessity; weight vs. lightness; emptiness vs. meaning . . . Speaking of emptiness, there was a time today when my whole body felt completely devoid of life and utterly without meaning. A character in one of Edith Wharton's novels says that "the real loneliness comes from all these kind faces who only ask one to pretend . . ." That is how I felt today, waiting anxiously for my afternoon pick-up, only to be let down, and later, facing the world (as if everything was okay inside). I apologize for having changed something.

Moth

March 3

Dear B—

I have thought some more about this concept of polarity that's been troubling you. It seems to relate to *string theory*, which gets its name from the assertion that the basic building block of the universe, the portion that cannot be further subdivided into another smaller particle, is an incredibly tiny vibrating string. And if string theory really is the TOE, "theory of everything" – then it has to be able to address issues physics never touches on, like love and art.*

---

* See Schrag, Robert L., *The God Chord: String Theory in the Landscape of the Heart*.

Consider yourself and the cello: As you play the music moves out to the listener, and also enters the core of your own being, for somehow you are tuned to the cello. Well, I am persuaded that this is because you ARE a chord. I AM a chord. Our DNA dictates our physicality – made up of billions of little notes – on a basic level. Add to that our geography, background, etc., and you have your original score. Then, everything we do, think and choose causes physiological differences in our minds and hearts or alters our score. Life is the layering of chords, but the underlying *one that we are* will never change. This brings us to string theory and love. Our personal chord resonates with the personal ones of others, and sometimes we encounter another person who is completely harmonious with us. It is a dominant, overwhelming attraction on the DNA level. However, such a person can *appear* to be our opposite – and that's where this 'opposites attract' notion comes from – because they have tuned their chord in a different way. In reality, we are attracted to the person we have chosen *not* to become, an alternative adjustment to a chord that is nearly the same as our own. The clashing portions of the chords sounding together advance the richness of it. So when you make love you aren't expressing emotions or showing affection, you are merging melodies. You are players in the same symphony.

Moth

M,
So THAT is what you think about in your lab all day? Why
don't you ever let me in?
B

April 9

My dearest B——

My god, it's been a day – soon to be two days since we
last spoke! Are you all right? Did you die? Are you stuck
by the side of the road, curling? Those heavy stones will
break your back and you'll fall on the ice. Oh, H-urling,
like, with an H. Never mind. I hadn't heard from you in
so long I assumed you were just blowing me off, well that
would be all right you know the . . . Me? Oh, I'm fine, solid
as a rock. No problem. Hangin' in, crazy as a loon.

Moth

April 11

Dear Moth,
Perhaps it is a common affliction of the synesthete, but I
believe I am just one pearl on a string, among many other,
past or future, bright, beautiful women who, I suspect,
adored you or will adore you as I adore you – and though
you say you have stopped *here*, I know you could never be
satisfied. You are more like me than you profess; so your
fingers will keep travelling along, one to the next. So you
will never realize that I am the true pearl among fakes –

and you'll move on, because you don't *see* me . . . You don't even know what you're looking for.

B.

April 12

Oh Butterfly—

The hail is pattering on the roof of my lab – a primordial sound. Water marks the most important moments, dreams and memories of my life. I have a confession to make: your heart entered mine during the blizzard that night seven years ago when you were not even there. I imagined you so clearly in my mind and looked for you everywhere. Then, four months ago you came into my life again, the woman who had visited me whenever it stormed – perhaps because you are unbelievably unpredictable from day to day.

You remain a mystery to me my love, so never believe I am bored with you, or presume I know you. Nor do you know me as well as you would believe. You are closer to my soul than any person has come before, but there is always another layer to the love and the lover. I look forward to unfolding you, continuously. There is no one else. It's all in the cold past.

Your Moth

P.S. And then there is your habit of elevating those around you to a level somehow more exalted than your own. "Ah," thought the butterfly, "if only I could be as swiftly nimble as the sparrows. They turn so swiftly, chatter so gregariously. There are so many of them! Surely they must be right about most things!" It is sometimes lonely being the butterfly, my love, but you are the most noticeable of all flying creatures, and you alight lives everywhere. You cannot become a sparrow — it is a waste of time to try.

May 29

Dear M,

I am still weak and sleepy, and have lost another ten pounds today — but have learned my lesson- and stopped taking those pills. I apologize for being so up-in-the-air about everything, but it was impossible to face you yesterday. It is necessary for me right now to lead by my mind instead of my heart. Let me tell you: I am considering a move back to Colorado. Seeing you again, talking with you, holding you, would make that impossible to express. What we have has an unfathomable power.

Butterfly

PS. I think you are rubbing off on me. Tonight I made banana bread for my son, who asked why it is called "bonanza" bread. I said, because every time you bite into it, it starts humming a tune. So when he took his first bite, I proceeded to hum the old TV theme from Bonanza . . . Then he said, "You're weird, Mommy."

May 29

B—

OK, I admit it, I'm pissed off. You led me to believe that you would be at the café yesterday morning, and you never showed up, never called and now answer my e-mail with THIS. In your mind you may have already left, but I have issues – no, more than that, I have questions you need to answer or you'll regret it, maybe not today or tomorrow, but for the rest of your life. Your excuse wasn't good enough.

Moth

May 30

Dear Butterfly—

I am not upset that you called and yelled at me as I finished my dinner. I was glad, in a weird way. I had this football coach who used to say, "I wouldn't give a cup a' warm spit for a kid who won't give a hundred percent." (And they say there are no more poets.) Anyhow, I wouldn't give a cup a' warm spit for someone who didn't yell and scream a bit when someone they love is cruel. I apologize for my rather inelegant comments. There is nothing so pathetic as a man standing in the middle of a prairie trying to call back the rain. I'd like to settle for nothing less than passion. You swept into my life in the midst of a blizzard seven years ago, but now it is only snow clouds along the horizon; and the storm can no more stay than the man can call it back . . .

I know you want to take your blizzard elsewhere. But think twice, and if so, I hope you find what you are looking for.
  M.

May 31

Dear M,

Ouch, that kind of hurts . . . Anyway, as I said before, this isn't about us, this is about me . . . And I do wish I could save you from myself – the me that is wavering, fickle, unsure, passionate, duplicitous, impatient, intense . . . Trust me on this one: your life would be easier.

Life for me is an unfolding artwork. Much of my confusion results from the fact that at the moment I am unsure, metaphorically, of the medium. Should I limit myself to the novel, or attempt poetry? I'm not sure. All I know is that it is supposed to be joyous and it isn't right now. At least I know the palette I should be employing. Perhaps that is progress. I know that there is a naturalistic theme that unfolds in my artwork. Storms are important metaphors for my life – but from a Zen-like perspective. Storms don't destroy, they replenish, nourish. But you cannot control them.*

Butterfly

_____

* Nature takes delight in nature; nature contains nature; and nature can overcome nature – Hermetic formula.

June 21

Dear Bfly—

You have asked me many times how I know I love you. You reminded me again today of a particularly telling way. I know because you can hurt me so. Pleasure is fairly easy to give – I can make people I barely know happy, but only people you love can hurt you and bring deep and torment- ing pain. Not flashing anger, the embarrassment of rejection from one you are getting to know or attempting to capture; the kind of pain that is surprising in its swiftness and inten- sity. I learned again today how quickly you can reach out and run your nails across my heart; and though I forgive you as soon as you tell me "sorry," the pain remains and laughter comes through the tears. It is not the joyous laughter from wanting you and loving you and knowing I was in return. This laughter is at myself, after learning that you took it and carried it to someone else, for continuing to believe that you want me and curse myself for doubting you. And then I laugh again because I still love you though you are fickle and take me for granted. Because I take joy in loving you even as you, through your words, abuse me.

You are right when you said, "This isn't about us, this is about me." It is about you, because until you love yourself there will be no us. Until that time you will continue to need losers to lust after you, and in their desire to have sex with you demonstrate that you have asserted your power over them and provided a fleeting spurt of evidence that you are *worth* loving. But it doesn't prove that to you at all, really, does it? Because you continue to hate yourself through another and another. For the love of yourself, stop. You have harder questions to answer.

Mo

June 24

Dearest M,
Once in a while my heart becomes so full it needs to open up and let the flood out, and sometimes it releases at the wrong moment, to the wrong person.
B.

P.S.: It would have been nice if you rescued me from duplicity. You know that I want to see you before I go . . .

June 26

Dear Butterfly—
There are these pivotal points in your life when you fall down Alice's rabbit hole and find yourself significantly changed. You seem, right now, to see yourself as being a different entity than you were before. I would argue not – with one of those concepts that needs a chapter: Duality. Two cultures: one knows H_2O only in its frozen form – ice. The other knows it only in its liquid form – water. The two cultures devise uses, definitions, stories, etc., utilizing their own conception of H_2O, unaware of its duality (that

in different conditions it takes on radically different characteristics). You are discovering one of your dualities. You are neither this Butterfly, or a previous one, alone — you are the sum of all of your Butterflies, and are best understood as having the characteristics of all your dualities expressed with selective dominance in a variety of situations.

My problem right now is that the sum of all my Moths is slowly accumulating into this scrapbook and I cannot find the structure to spring me free. It is strange — I really want you to love me, understand me, challenge me, and allow me to do the same for you, but to do that you have to know Moth in all his dualities, and he is locked up in a stupid scrapbook.

   Moth

June 29

Darling Mo,

What is a four-letter word that begins with E and ends with D meaning "Holy Cow"?

What is a six-letter word that begins with T and ends with D, meaning "Fed"?

What is a five-letter word meaning "no good," begins with L and is not loser?

B.

July 1

Oh Moth,

I am feeling so much the way I felt that day when the snapshot was taken of me in the cemetery. I am numb, for some reason, while being constantly aware of every tiny thing that sweeps by me — a needle making tiny pricks all over my body. Please understand why I must go. Be sure that if now I were given my choice to have known you or not known you — despite the wrongness of it — a thousand times I would claim to keep what I have. I cannot forget that for seven months I was the happiest woman alive — you claimed my soul, and it had never been alive as it was with you. Our relationship has made me feel more myself than ever before, but strangely, has also made me feel part of *a larger whole*, among many other true lovers in history throughout the world. Everything in love has been done before, in various times and places. We can see ourselves in their stories, and they in ours.

Butterfly

July 7

Dearest Butterfly—

Without asking your permission, I put my happiness and yours in your sweet but REALLY UNSTABLE keeping. If you screw it up and choose not to return, I will create some really beautiful art designed to reflect the life you and I could have created. I would prefer to create that art with you: *and so faith allows you to believe that not only will she return but through an unbelievable miracle, loves you.*

Moth

Hi Moth,
I would like to ask you some questions that will help me in my packing job. Please answer fully & honestly.

— Do you know how to fill holes in plaster, i.e., like in my wall?
— What should I do with the big mirror that goes with my desk?
— Do you think I should take my cacti?
— What the heck am I doing?

B.

B—

— Sort of, depends how big.
— Either store it or accidentally drop it (a sign of good luck in Russia).
— I doubt it. Too prickly.
— Moving into the next chapter of your life. You would have had to do it even if you stayed here. It will be all right.

Moth

July 10

Darling B—

I need to cry and mourn the passing of emotional sweetness and overwhelming love. Maybe I always think of you in a blizzard because you could never have been domesticated in a day-to-day life. Try not to think of me as the man you fell out of love with. Remember me as the man who took you to see the sundogs in Alberta, who taught you to smoke cigars in a chalet in Switzerland, who came running to England whenever you tried to hurt yourself. I will keep in my heart the woman whose smile would light the room when I walked in, whose loving could remove all the bones from my body, whose writing continues to touch my soul. The Grand Canyon will miss you. I do so love to ride the storm – it hurts to see it pass. Look to your own heart, my darling girl. Think of your own safety and comfort. Choose wisely.

Moth

December 3

Sweet Butterfly—

Forgive me, but I had to write you – you are really on my shoulder this morning. First I went into the café – I know; we had some wonderful times there so I just go and sit and smile and remember. God the place is a wreck! The back rooms look empty, all the display cases are empty or half empty. Some girl I've never seen was working the counter – and even though she did very nice things to her CyberVision T-Shirt and tight blue jeans I wanted her gone! The place seems to be dying. Then I picked up the *Wall Street Journal* – little sidebar story on Colorado:

"A light snow this morning pushed Aspen's snow total for the season over 100 inches – the earliest the city has ever broken that barrier." Brrrr! I thought – my girl must be freezing. Hope you are doing well there. I dread each minute that passes without feeling your breath on my cheek or seeing you smile.*

Moth

December 7

Dear Moth,

I AM freezing, but I'm not in Colorado anymore. I finished my book and somehow I found myself getting on a plane and travelling to even colder climes – first to Oslo, where I saw tall Norwegians with beautifully clear skin, horns on head, and heard cheering, ringing cowbells. After that, Finland for two days: clean, quiet, orderly and cold. Now I find myself in Russia: art, music, architecture, potholes below, icicles above, and pickpockets on all sides.

I visited Patriarch's Ponds – one large body of water that forms the heart of a square surrounded by wrought-iron railings and mature trees. Of course, there were my strolls through Red Square, The Kremlin, St Basil's Cathedral and Gorky Park, which made me feel so far away from you. Still

---

* "We were together / Only a little while, / And we believed our love / Would last a thousand years." – Yakamochi (718–85).

I dream of the falling, falling snow, a candle flame, shadows on the wall, the chill of your lips, wet hair and cold toes, and the warmest embrace.
Butterfly

See PSYCHE & COLOUR　　*Moth and Butterfly, Crimea*

Further reading: Seba, Albertus, *Locupletissimi Rerum Naturalium Thesauri Accurata Descriptio*, Amsterdam, 1760.

❅

ICE is frozen water often having an opaque appearance and shiny surface, usually in a contained form, i.e.: as cubes in a cherry soda, as a skating rink in Central Park, Manhattan. I slipped my hand into my father's hand, wearing puffy gloves. I used him for balance. Soon I'd be making figure eights, skirt twirling, ponytail swirling, just like the older girls. But for now I stepped lightly, like dipping my right toe into a pool of water to test the temperature, one skate at a time, new to the territory. *One, two, three, push! One, two, three, push!* Dad chanted alongside me. I followed his voice then whispered, *Shhh, Dad . . . You're embarrassing me.* He stopped chanting.

Around the enormous Christmas Tree we went, seeing every ornament, ball and star amidst the pine, on the occasions we looked over for a tiny glimpse, for fear either of us would slip up and pull the other down too. Dad was cautious as a beginner. He wobbled on his skates, awkwardly, and his feet moved outward as if he would attempt a split. This sight made me uneasy, but he'd told me he was almost a professional and I believed him. *Come on, Dad. Let's go faster!* I suggested. *I don't think that's a good idea, Francis,* he replied. *You're not ready yet.* Everyone was wearing brightly colored hats, otherwise striped, or with knitted balls – some holding hands, others flying solo with arms moving, *swish, swish.* There were carolers all dressed in red wool, holding songbooks and hymning "Silent Night." Dad finally quickened our steps, and the next time I was gliding instead of stepping – actually gliding! – then I let go of Dad's hand but stayed near, then I was flying along the ice far from him, and later, moving backwards and doing figure eights, skirt twirling, blonde ponytail swirling and Dad was nowhere to be seen.

See WINK & WHISTLE   *F. Ferguson, N. Jersey*

❄

IMPATIENCE. We live near the North Sea in a castle where the wind often makes itself known. At night I listen to it blow down the long corridors, and my entire body is shaken by an unwelcome trembling. Oh inconstant heart, my imagination has misled me! I am so anxious to take possession of it once more, to throw away my winding sheets as much as the dead in the graves are impatient to raise their stones and live again. If only you could trespass my imaginary universe like a walk into fire* . . . If only you knew me and loved me!

G. de Staël, Switzerland

❉

JOURNEY on a train from Moscow to Varykino: my family and I watched the smooth snow lit in front of the first car as the train, moving at a snail's pace, reached the village of Lower Kelmes. The men climbed out of the train compartments and stamped their boots in the snow. They'd had a blizzard for an entire week in Lower Kelmes and its surroundings, leaving snowdrifts along the stretch of railway and blowing in great drifts. We wanted to go on to reach our destination, as the children were restless, but first we were petitioned to help the workmen of the village. The men divided into two groups while the women and children remained inside the train compartment, huddled together in the hay. We formed two groups on either side of the large snow mounds and began to dig and hurl. The deepest part was in the middle of the line. It took us three days to clear that line! I remember this now, at the finale of winter. My

---

* "In the bleak mid-winter, frosty wind made moan . . ." "Come to me in the silence of the night, in the speaking silence of a dream." – Christina Rossetti (1830–94).

God, already it is April, and Varykino has been cleansed by a thunderstorm! It's the finale of blizzards, of cold, months during which I stayed indoors, caught rheumatism and shaved my beard every day. I remember this now. Those were the best days of that journey from Moscow.

Y. Andreyevich, Varykino

❄

KISS, occurring when two persons or things fade into one another by locking lips or caressing noses. My first kiss was at fifteen with a man of fifty-three named Nanuq (Polar Bear), who sold pelts and whale blubber. I could see his breath form in the air when he spoke to me, trying to make a sale. Every week I saw him. "No, thank you," I said. "No furs, thank you." Nanuq invited me to his peat-constructed igloo by raising his hand to the side: *Follow me.* I trudged behind him in the snow. We mounted his dogsled and set off. If we were travelling on snowshoes, the journey would have taken longer. The distance was five miles. Nanuq lived alone, built fires alone, dined alone on smoked fish: one mat for sleeping, one Loonskin coat, one slate-seal knife. When we sat inside on the straw floor, Nanuq leaned close to me, though we were already cosy enough in the compacted space. He blinked the snow on his lashes and put his face up to mine. He touched the tip of my nose with his, which was surprisingly warm. I sniffled. He held his eyes in an open gaze as he grazed my nose, moving the tip back and forth

with soft nudges. He sniffed me, holding his nostril to one
of mine, breathed me in.

 See UUKKARNIT   ***Massak, Alaska***

❄

LEGEND:
You are JÜŠTƏ ERGE, the winter-child spirit that is heard
on cold nights bouncing a ball off doors and roofs of houses.
You call out in the darkness for the other children to join
you, but when they do not, you steal into their houses to
nip at their fingers and toes. You are FATHER FROST, a
powerful blacksmith who binds the earth and the oceans in
chains of ice. You control all the glacial formations of the
globe. You are the JÜŠTƏ KUGUZA, the old couple who
rattle fences and stumbles pedestrians in the snow. You are
relentless in your pursuit of warm-blooded people. You are
one of the SEVEN STARS OF PLEIADES, the seven sisters, so cold that you sparkle with icicles. Once a year you
pull flowers of ice from your body and cast them to the
earth. You are JÜŠTƏ MUŽƏ, a demon who inflicts chills
on humans. You cause them to have shivering fits that take
possession of their bodies and kill the nerves of their teeth,
splitting them to pieces. You are HRIMTHURSAR,
descended from the giant Ymir. You are a sculpture of ice.
You are YUKI-ONNE, the Snow Woman, who appears
during a whiteout. You lure men to sleep and death, but first
you have your way with them.

                  Ed.

LOST, Hello?
. . . *Hello, hello, hello* . . .
Is anybody out there?
. . . *out there, out there* . . .

Capt. Oates, South Pole

❋

MAN, "Abominable Snow," also known as Yeti. An absolute beast I tell you! An indefinable, big stinking exotic animal with long dark fur and 11-feet tall on two feet. You wouldn't believe your eyes. I came face-to-face with him one night in the Tibetan Wilderness in 1986, where I was cycling. Did I say cycling? No, no . . . hiking, of course; and it was '87, but anyway, I stood there in front of him, frozen like a sculpture, just waiting for him to do something; kill me, anything.* But he got down on all fours and ran away quickly.

L. Williams, South Tyrol

❋

---

* The need to meet, postpone or overcome death yields symbolism of suffering and resurrection and, in alchemy, the quest for the life spirit of things.

MATERIA PRIMA, a.k.a. the Stone of the Philosophers, the *quinta essentia*, or the ultimate goal in alchemy. Painting, like alchemy, is about creating mixtures, an ongoing negotiation between stone and water. The quest for *Materia Prima** by the artist is called the Great Work, or *Magnum Opus*, as the whole of the Work is prepared and achieved with this substance. *Materia Prima* is, above all, the moment of silence before the beginning of the Work, the calm before the storm. What a silence it is! From the very beginning of the Work we must assume we have obtained the hidden chaos of *Materia Prima*, our own chaos. It is similar to the beginning of the world in Genesis, before the separation of all things into distinct elements – a world balancing precariously on confusion. Similarly, in painting, we must fight against uniformity and shape. The idea is to continue overlapping, jabbing and stroking so that each mark is different. The Work should, therefore, be chaos: a swirl of glints and angles, with everything that tumbles together so

---

* *Materia Prima* is a substance said to have an imperfect body, constant soul, penetrating tincture and transparent mercury of the wise. In alchemical texts, it is called by many names, but my favourites are, among them, the silent and cold:

A White Moisture	Pure Virgin	Chaos
Crystal		White Smoke
Glass	Shade of the Sun	

you forget yourself and what you are creating. The Work should become comforting and circular . . . with a sweep of the hand a streak of Vermilion descends on the canvas and leaves a streaming trail over the layers of Cerulean Blue and Lead White. Flashes of yellow and flying white drag along the silk but, when stepping back, become tangled up in blue.

See SHROUD   *C. Monet, Vétheuil*

❄

MOON:

MARE FRIGORIS – The Sea of Cold
OCEANUS PROCESSARUM – The Ocean of Storms
LACUS SOMNIORUM – The Lake of Dreamers
SINUS RORIS – The Bay of Dews
LACUS MORTIS – The Lake of Death
MARE CRISIUM – The Sea of Pain
PALUS SOMNII – The Marsh of Sleep

W. Blake, England

❄

NAGA NAGASHI YO*

I.

A host of streamers
Flicker and glitter,
Quiver and tremble,
An aurora in the sky.

II.

Snow is on statues
Of river-gods in gardens.
His white hair on my pillow
Is a token of his love.

III.

My inconstant heart
Floats in the Lake of Taunitz.
I leave it behind.

IV.

After the first frost
Do you feel me in the mist
On Fujiyama

---

* 'the long, long night'

Where I am waiting for you,
Under the mid-autumn moon?

V.

Without my lover
The wind is a lasting tomb.
The days are frozen.

VI.

A woven meadow
Of pear tree petals
Leaves behind beauty
And fewer traces of grief.

VII.

I will come to you
At the River of Heaven.
I will wait for you,
With the night falling away
And my heart full of courage.*

See TESTIMONY   *Lady-in-Waiting to the*
                           Empress Ulu, Naniwa Bay

---

* "Deliverance from that death, the death of the wombe, is an entrance, a delivering over to another death." – John Donne, *Deaths Duell*.

NAKED: Pure and transparent like the moon & clouds & whiteness of snow

When I walked down the corridor at high school, the fluorescent lights cast the same harsh glow over healthy faces as they did over sick ones at the hospital where I worked. The same ammonia scent lingered in the air. And the disembodied voices called "Ms. Somebody to somewhere," instead of "Dr. Somebody to somewhere – stat;" but here I wasn't on my way to reach out to someone, bring a smile to a face, here I was hollow and alone, clinging to the wall.

When I reached the locker that I shared with my best friend Libby, I zipped through the combination, hoping for a note from her or some little token to compel me through the morning. And there it was on our dry erase board, surrounded by a hodge-podge of art postcards, pictures of musicians, writers and freedom fighters. *All your hard work paid off. I feel I should launch fireworks or have a parade in your honor. I'm so proud of you. xxx. L.*

I smiled, but what did she mean?

Someone nudged my shoulder, and I whipped around to greet Libby. But it wasn't her. Rather, it was the guy from my Russian class, the one with a coifed flame of red hair (dyed), a hoop nose ring and a perfect set of front teeth. We'd never spoken before, but I knew his name was Drew. *Why was he here?*

"Did you draw me a picture on my table in the cafeteria?" he asked.

"What?" I had to think a moment. "Um, yes." I had, in fact, drawn a picture of a bumblebee on a cafeteria table last week while eating a dream bar, whether or not it was his table I didn't know — at least not consciously. I certainly hadn't sketched it *for him*.

"Well, thanks. You're very good," he said. "Do you weld too?" He towered over me with a rumpled sort of legginess. His hands shook as he held his books, but otherwise he didn't appear nervous. Maybe he was on a caffeine buzz.

"Um, yes," I lied. Then, "Why? Want me to weld you something when I have the time?"

He nodded and went on flashing his big whites. "Actually, I just bought this Massai warrior movie and I thought you'd like to watch it with me."

What? First of all, this was a guy who always had women coffee-talking of his tall gracefulness, striking intellect and endless creativity. Second, he was always seen with the tall, primarily clad in black, Germaine (AND she was French). Third, how did he know I was interested in the Massai?

"Hmmm."

"Walk with me to Russian?" he asked.

I looked around to see if Libby was coming. She wasn't. "Okay."

We walked down the hallway, merging with the crowd that poured out of the lunchroom. Recognizable faces, some my friends, looked at us as if we were some strange breed. After all, to them he was Drew Davidson — philosopher and prodigy – and I was just Paulina – poet and prude. They waved and raised eyebrows.

". . . So try to call me tonight," he was saying. "We could talk politics, or the weather, love and marriage – whatever."

My binder banged against his and I blushed.

"My number is 863-9102," he said. "My old number was 863-2415, but don't call that one because I'm not sure who owns that telephone now."

"Okay." We reached the classroom. Suddenly, an arm slipped around my waist and I turned.

It was Libby.

"Hi sweetie," she said, moving her face close to mine and ignoring my male companion.

"Hi . . . got your note. Where've you been?"

Drew stood in our classroom doorway, smiling at me. He shrugged and disappeared into the room. His sudden attention was unsettling.

"I heard the news . . . You're wonderful . . ." Libby purred.

"What news? What do . . . ?"

She clapped a hand over her mouth. "Oh! You don't know?"

I shook my head.

"Oops! Well, I saw Ms. Paul this morning and she . . . well, I'm sure Harvey will call you to the office sometime today, then."

"Lib, what's going on?"

"Nothing!" She squeezed my cheeks and puckered her lips, kissing the air. "Go to class. I'll see you later."

She pranced away, a pink skirt swishing against the back of her long, slender thighs, sleek black hair brushing her shoulders, arms swinging – all movements like a synchronous pendulum. When she rounded the corner, I missed her already.

Sure enough, Mr. Harvey sent me a pass during psychology class. When I got to the principal's office, first he made nervous chitchat, then he paused and leaned forward with folded hands across the desk.

"You're our Salutatorian, Paulina."

I flushed. He could be mistaken. Maybe they were too hasty in tallying the grades. I wasn't that smart. "Really?"

"Absolutely. In fact, it was real close."

"Who's Valedictorian?" I asked on impulse. But before he answered, I already knew what he'd say.

"Drew."

"Wonderful."

I looked out the window at the clouds shifting through the sky and the dark invading the light: all things familiar – the concrete, the yellow buses, the stars-n-stripes waving in the wind. I was a foreigner trapped in a strange country, without the language. *Who are these people? What have I been doing here for all these years? Salutatorian, is that really me?*

"You probably know you'll have to give a speech at graduation. The sooner you write it, the better for you."

A speech? I have to stand in front of a thousand people and open my mouth? When will I even get the time to write it?

"Great! Thank you, sir. Well, I'd better get back to class."

"We're real proud of you, Paulina — and I hope everything is going okay at home."

"Just fine, sir," I lied, and rushed out.

After school, Libby and I went to her house before I had to rush to my job at the hospital. She poured us two celebratory glasses of merlot and we climbed the stairs to her bedroom/art studio in the attic. We liked to go there because her dad was always working and we could be alone hugging our shared secrets. Her room was littered with books and clothes, her studio with brushes and canvases. She put on an Elvis Costello CD as I made myself comfortable on her futon. We lay side-by-side atop her daisy sheets, looking up at the skylight and holding hands — two healthy, firm sets of fingers clutching one another confidently. I wished to feel excited, hopeful, even anxious, but I felt as skeletal as Libby had looked in the hospital the first few days of our companionship. My writing, my distracted father and my mother's absence poked inside me like bony ribs bruising my racing heart.

"It'll be all right, honey," Libby whispered.

"No it won't."

Libby propped her head on her left hand and began stroking my hair, watching me with her doe-like hazel eyes.

Her top and bottom eyelashes stuck together for a short moment each time she blinked. They looked like tangled insect legs, but sexier.

"I don't want this Salutatorian thing. It's not even *me*. I should have quit school a long time ago."

She sipped her wine. "And write?"

"Yes. Move to somewhere warm, like New Mexico. Write poetry on a mesa."

"You *are* a writer here," she said, swallowing. "What about me? You don't love me." She thrust out her full bottom lip in a pout that I knew so well.

"Of course I do. You're the only one who keeps me sane."

"Miss your Mom?"

"Yeah. It's only been seven months and I can't remember the way she looked anymore."

"You'll see each other again . . ."

"Do you think so?"

Libby nodded.

My whole body burned, lying there in the stuffiness of the attic with the sun beaming down on us from above. There had been so many moments like these, with Libby, since we met two years before: moments when the space between us diminished to hardly nothing, so that I didn't know where I ended and she began. Moments when I thought we might melt into one another, as we managed to creep closer and closer, but prevented ourselves from merging.

I breathed in her scent of ylang-ylang and juniper and stared at the wall. Tall Klimt women, swirled in embraces, looked back at me.

She stared at me like she had a recent revelation. "You look like Kim Novak with your hair pulled back," she said. "We should dye it platinum. What do you think?"

"I don't know. Maybe. My Dad would kill me."

"Let it go. He can't rule you forever."

Dad was all I had left. But she was right again: I'd always been a puppet to my parents, teachers, friends, and hated them for it, but most of all hated myself for having lived that way. A stranger to self, like a character in a book that I identified with and genuinely wanted to know, but couldn't. I wanted to cut my strings and break out on my own, but I was too frightened that once I did, I'd be tripping and straggling over them.

Libby had her eyes closed. I inched toward her and wrapped my arms around her, pulling tighter and tighter. Then, the phone rang. We sat for a moment, listening to the sound of our heavy breathing, until I moved away from her and she grabbed the phone.

"Hello . . . Yes, sir . . . Yes, sir . . . Okay, she's leaving right now," Libby said into the receiver. Then, she hung up.

She didn't have to tell me it was Dad calling to find out why I wasn't home for dinner yet.

"You'd better go. He sounded pissed." Libby was sprawled out on the futon.

"You're an angel, you know that?" I said. She looked at me with a blank stare, as if I was an apparition. She did that when she was trying not to cry. Then she lit a cigarette and puffed away, blowing smoke rings at me as I turned and walked away.

When I got home, Pop was standing in the hallway, near the kitchen.

"You're late," he said gruffly.

"I know. Sorry, Libby and I . . ."

He cut me off. "You spend too much time with that girl. I don't like it. She's trouble."

Any guilt that I felt for what passed between Libby and I quickly vanished. I felt icy. Defiant. "I like spending time with her. She's my friend."

"Family's more important."

I stared at him.

He drummed his fingers on the counter, impatiently. "How was school? Anything interesting happen today?"

"No," I mumbled. "Nothing at all."

* * *

Lookit, I gotta boo-boo, I would say. *Mommy, I gotta boo-boo.*

Mmm, poor baby, Mommy would say, not turning away from boiling artichokes, simmering angel hair or stewing tomatoes. *Go clean up the doggie crap in the foyer,* she'd add, or *Hurry up and do your homework so we can go shopping.*

I went to Daddy. *Daddy, look! I've gotta boo-boo!* I would

say, flaunting a wound on my arm or my leg or whatever appendage was hurt at the time, all from those unintentional falls. He'd turn to me slowly, putting down his tools, *How'd you get to be such a klutz? Huh?* He'd turn away and focus on a project as the blood oozed from the cut in my skin. The tears flowed easily then, so easy that Daddy would say, *Fer chrissake, don't be such a crybaby!*

So I went elsewhere. It didn't take long to realize that I craved attention, and if Daddy and Mommy couldn't give it to me, someone would. When I was fifteen I found that someone, who would understand the tears and the pain and the blood and say, in a crooning tone, *Oh baby doll, let me lick those for you . . .*

Of course, that someone was Libby.

The first time I saw her she was 70 pounds, feeding from an IV and doing both group and art therapy at the institution as treatment for anorexia nervosa and bulimia. I was going through my helping-out stage at the time, volunteering for the hospital in the ward for young women with depression and other mental illnesses. But it wasn't until Libby that I realized these women weren't all "freaks" and "psychos" like I originally thought. Actually, most of them were a lot like me – feeling unloved or neglected, wanting to live out their dreams but without courage, trying to take control of their lives by any means, even if it meant starving themselves to the edge of death.

I was another soul who needed saving and Libby was the

one who recognized it, plucked me off the altar and rescued me – my angel, my little star.

When I walked into her room the first day her fabulous paintings were all over the walls: plump, nude women* who looked so sad, with dark eyes and tangles of hair. One woman in particular caught my eye, the darkest queen of them all, and I could not tear my eyes away.

"That's me," she said weakly, lopsided on her back, hands tucked under her buttocks to ease the pain of sitting on bones. Her short black hair framed her face like wilted spinach and her eyes bulged as if in constant surprise.

"That's you?" I studied the painting again and recognized Libby's Hungarian nose and pouty lips, but then the large hips . . . "You're kidding."

"A self-portrait," she said, baring her huge white teeth.

"I hope it's a premonition."

"What do you mean?"

"You'd look great with a few more pounds on . . ."

"I look a lot bigger than that now," she said. "They're making me fat here. I hate it."

"Have you looked in the mirror lately?"

---

* "To be naked is to be oneself. To be nude is to be seen naked by others and yet not recognized for oneself. A naked body has to be seen as an object in order to become a nude . . . To be naked is to be without disguise . . . The nude is condemned to never being naked. Nudity is a form of dress." – John Berger, *Ways of Seeing*.

"No, and I'm sure you mean well, but you don't even know me so who are you to say?"

"You're right," I said. "What would I know?"

She rested her head against the pillow, avoiding my eyes. She had a look of resignation on her face, like she could continue suffering without feeling a thing. A child, really, but almost an old woman. She wore a silver-beaded chain around her neck, plastic and worn. In my head I walked over and ran it through my two fingers. Instead, I dropped some magazines on her bedside table and went to the next room on my route.

I should've told her I'd see her tomorrow, I thought. She probably guessed I'd return.

The rest of my shift I couldn't stop thinking of the girl. Nothing had ever moved me so much as the sight of her, even though most of the women in there had it pretty bad.

As I walked back from the hospital toward my house, each step seemed to separate me from something vital. All that evening the talking and laughter of my family reached me as if I was underwater and trying to swim my way to the surface. Shadows and reflections moved along the walls in slow-motion replay, and I could hear only faint sounds, like ripples. Eventually I fled to my bed, but was constantly aware of the time as I tried to sleep. The house echoed with TV broadcasts from downstairs and I imagined Mom and Dad fiddling with the rabbit-ear antennae on top of the set. Soon they were having an argument about the bad signal.

I heard Mom's exclamation: *Snow again!* And Daddy's reply: *I'm tired of this snow.* Finally slipping into sleep, my dreams carried images of dismembered bodies: painfully thin people without heads or arms, legs or hands or feet, emaciated forms of disturbing beauty.

The next day after school, I went straight to the hospital. When I walked into the girl's room she was looking out the window at the falling snow. Her face lit up when she saw me — a good sign. I carried in a full-length mirror, and propped it against the far wall. She had replaced the dull white hospital bed sheets with collage-like modern ones.

"Nice sheets," I said.

"Thanks, my boyfriend got 'em for me."

Our eyes met and we stared at each other for a while, until she fidgeted in her bed and broke the spell. "They're actually a forgive-me kind of gift," she told me. "He's a real idiot."

"Why? Did he do something wrong?"

"Well, he slept with my mother."

I stepped back and shook my head. "Damn. So give the sheets back."

She smiled, pulled out her IV and eased off the bed, squinting so I knew it hurt. She was barefoot, wearing a white T-shirt and boxer shorts, legs like twigs. I thought they might crack in half as her feet, purple from poor circulation, hit the floor.

"What's the mirror for?" she asked.

"Thought I'd give your day a change of pace," I said.

"Good. The only people that come in here are nurses checking to see if I've vomited, gone diarrhea or screwed with my IV."

She's glad I'm here, I thought. *Let's hope it stays that way.* I ran to the door, closed it, and kept my back to her.

"Uh . . . take off your clothes," I said.

She cleared her throat nervously, then the room got quiet and I waited. Her clothes brushed against her body slowly like a tiny waterfall in the distance. Her feet began to patter across the room. I imagined her naked, standing in front of the mirror and assessing her body as I did mine in the mornings fresh out of the shower.

"What do you see?"

"Err," she said. "I see my mother."

"Oh? How?"

"Her hips, her huge round hips."

"That's not what other people see . . . So why do you?"

"Because I *am* my mother."

"No you're not. Besides, that's a cop-out."

"You sound like my therapist."

"Well, I guess I've had some personal experience with this kind of thing," I confessed.

"Therapy?" she asked.

"No, mothers."

She was silent for a moment. I had the urge to turn around – talking to the wall was becoming difficult.

She raised her voice. "Hey, turn around and look at me."

"Isn't that against the rules?"

"Isn't telling me to take my clothes off against the rules? Besides, you don't seem like the kind of girl who follows rules."

"Right," I mumbled.

Slowly, I turned around and was caught by the whiteness of her naked body, her flat chest, then her shaven pubic area, which made her look like a 12-year-old boy, but more striking was her emaciated frame – reminding me of cadavers I'd seen in Holocaust footage or commercials of starving children to whom you could donate $10 per month. Her skin was like a transparent sheath covering bones and blue veins. I closed my eyes, thinking I would cry or run screaming from the room.

Then I realized she was crying so I moved toward her and wrapped my arms around her skeletal frame. She trembled beneath my touch. Finally she hugged back, and the scent of ylang-ylang and juniper in her hair brushed my cheek.

"I don't know what to do . . ." she whispered as the tears dripped down the sides of her face.

"It's going to be okay." I patted her back.

After a few minutes, pulling away, she didn't budge, as if she were drowning in a sea and clutching a raft, so I let her hold me. Her eyes fluttered behind closed, parchment-thin lids. There was a purplish spot on her cheek that didn't wash away beneath the tears: it was in the same place as my chickenpox scar, just above the right cheekbone. I reached up and placed my finger on it, trying to wipe it away.

"It won't move," she told me. "It's always been there."

"Always?"

"Since my sister stabbed me with a pen," she said, clearing her throat.

"On purpose?"

"Yeah, it was one of those times she tried to kill me when I was a baby." She let go of me and backed away, shrugging. A stream of light rushed in through the window and caught on her hair, capturing its soft auburn tones. I wanted to tell her she was beautiful, truly beautiful, but she said it first.

"Gosh, you're really beautiful."

I blushed and turned away. "Thanks. Well, I'd better go." I turned toward the door. "I'll see you tomorrow."

"By the way, what's your name?" she asked, just as I was ready to round the corner.

"Paulina . . . What's yours?"

"Libby," she answered, her voice rising as if I should've known.

"Nice to meet you," I said, winked, and went out the door.

Walking along the hallway, my jeans made swishing sounds that were stifled by screams and shouts of neighboring patients. But the noise didn't bother me as it usually did; the blend of cries suddenly sounded like a Beethoven symphony being played just slightly out of key. The calls for doctors, the lights, the tiles, the waxed floor, and the pungent smell, which previously were little pieces of a dismal passage that got me to the next place, came together and I saw life more clearly then, and somehow, more tangibly. That day all those pieces became a precious part of my own personal world.

See FRIGID   ***Paulina, an American in France***

❅

NATIVITY:

The Pavlovskis' Christmas Decoration Plan, for Oct 1–Feb 1 2001:

1. Bethlehem Nativity with Stable in front yard
2. Large Plastic Praying Angel, lit, on front porch
3. Sheep & Straw, everywhere possible while not spilling over into neighbor's territory (occasional slip-ups are allowed, i.e.: an angel's wing peeking out over the boundary line)
4. Strings of lights on all branches of two large elms in front yard, along with 8 trees in back yard. Lighting along the gutters of the house, along the rooftop and lining all 30 windows. Party-colored only. Install red glowing Santa Claus and the reindeer on slope of roof
5. Miniature Nativity in foyer
6. Tinsel and mistletoe, artificial snow and dry ice everywhere

7. Hire xylophone player
8. Decorate tree
9. Manger with Christ Child and Magi, imported from Germany, living room
10. Make fruitcake
11. Do assorted plastic flower arrangements in solstice colors
12. Sew monograms on stockings
13. Illuminate large crucifixion scene on garage door
14. Spike the eggnog

M. J. Pavlovski, Flamingo Trailer Park, Florida

✳

ORCHESTRAL. Reverend Antonius Vivaldi died 27/28 July 1741 in Satlerisch Haus near the Kärntner Tor. Body examined: 28 July. Cause of death: internal burning. Old: 60 Years. Expenses: 19 Gulden and 45 Kreuzer. Buried near St Charles Church, at Spitaller Gottesacker.

Protocol of the Deceased, Vienna

✳

PATRON: Thank heavens for people like Maecenas, who came along and converted my hill into beautiful gardens. This place was loathsome before: infested with banditti and cast-out bodies of plebeians that no one cared about. The heathens were thrown into profane sepulchres or ill-made coffins to putrefy; and the ground was a network of pits left by the sand diggers, covered with whitening bones. What a stink! Yes, thank heavens for Maecenas. Now I am grateful to live on the Esquiline, with a reed stuck on the top of my head to ward off troublesome birds and unwanted spirits. Go away, you buffoons!

Scarecrow, Rome

❄

POLAR-ITY:

COLD is a story about elements, opposites, loneliness, friendship . . . a story about love.

PLAYERS:

The Exhausted Mother

The Strong Father

The King

The Queen

Princess Fiammarosa, or the Icewoman

Hugh, the tutor

Prince Boris

Prince Sasan

The Snow

I. The Strong Father and The Exhausted Mother announce the birth of their thirteenth child (a most unusual girl)

Darkness and a high-pitched scream.

FATHER: What is it?

Lights, shades of red . . . a sunflower is placed in a red vase that is sitting on a small table behind the Mother and Father, who interlock hands, holding a baby together, gazing downward.

MOTHER: *Stammers.* F . . . F . . . F . . .

FATHER: Our first princess in a line of princes.

MOTHER: *Exhaustedly* . . . Fiammarosa!

FATHER: She is beautiful, and her hair is like black fur!

MOTHER: May we call her Fiammarosa, my King? She is so soft and gentle.

FATHER: She *is* a delicate child.

MOTHER: *Cradling the baby to her chest, she reveals her breast and pulls the baby to her.* Her skin is milky, like white rose petals.

FATHER: She is delicate like bone china. *To the baby, declaratively,* No one shall ever harm you, my child!

MOTHER: Look, my King, her eyes have no colour.

TOGETHER: . . . newborn blue.

FATHER: She must be kept warm.

MOTHER: Yes, she is so thin . . .

FATHER: And she must be well fed. *Pauses, raises a finger in thought, and says loudly,* Give her soups, meats, vegetables, custards and zabagliones!

MOTHER: Never was a girl loved more . . .

FATHER: There is no fault in her.

Father hands the baby to Mother and leaves the stage.

II. HUGH, THE TUTOR, BEGINS TO UNDERSTAND FIAMMAROSA AS SHE BLOSSOMS INTO A WOMAN (A VERY BEAUTIFUL ONE)

Light shines through a half-open window that hangs stage right. The table at centre now holds a red vase with a single sunflower. Stage left there is a desk stacked with papers, and next to it, a bookshelf filled with books of philosophy, fables, and novels of love and loss. Fiammarosa, now thirteen years old, is dressed in a long flowing dress and her blonde hair is in braids. Hugh enters wearing a three-piece suit and spectacles, holding an open book.

HUGH: *Facing his pupil.* What is it, Fiammarosa? Do you feel tired?

FIAMMAROSA: *Looking directly at Hugh.* No. Why should I? *Pause.* I feel much as usual.

HUGH: *Stays near the window, but turns to face Fiammarosa.* Did you read Stendhal, then?

FIAMMAROSA: Yes, Hugh.

HUGH: How does he define crystallisation?

FIAMMAROSA: He says that crystallisation can occur between two lovers, in their minds.

HUGH: Excellent . . . *Clapping his hands together.* What happens then?

FIAMMAROSA: When two lovers are parted the one in love will draw from everything new proofs of perfection in the other.

HUGH: *Approaching her.* Well done! Did you know that Stendhal fell in love with the Countess Viscontini? He confessed his love to the Countess but she would not hear him. Still, he flooded her with letters. Finally they came to an agreement that he could visit every fortnight for one hour in the presence of others. This arrangement lasted two years, during which his love grew so unbearable that he had to flee to Milan.

FIAMMAROSA: Why didn't she love him?

HUGH: *Shrugging.* Perhaps she was too cold.

The players freeze momentarily. The lights dim to darkness, then brighten again, gradually, signalling a new day.

HUGH: *Approaching the bookshelf.* Let's read the myth of St Eulalia today.

FIAMMAROSA: *Yawning.* But I'm so tired.

Hugh takes a book off the shelf and leafs through its pages.

HUGH: But she was a martyr. Who died in the snow!

FIAMMAROSA: . . . so tired.

HUGH: This is important for you, my dear. One day you are sharp and the next you are dull!

Fiammarosa collapses slowly on to the floor but he doesn't see her.

HUGH: Though I do not mind, if you need to rest . . . Yes, you should . . .

He turns to notice her on the floor, walks over and kneels. He touches her head, caressing her hair. His body collapses over hers. They are draped together. Darkness.

III. THE ICEWOMAN AND THE SNOW

The stage is bathed in blue light with one small table centre stage upon which is now a clear vase and a single white lily. The Icewoman stands near the window in a sheer nightgown and slippers.

SNOW: *A male's voice from offstage.* I am the snow that falls in the meadow.

ICEWOMAN: I can see lawns and bushes under snow, and the long tips of icicles pour down from the eaves above me. The full moon! It touches my window!

She puts her cheek to the window and closes her eyes.

SNOW: She adheres to me ever so slightly.

ICEWOMAN: The ice seizes my cheek!

She removes her cheek from the glass, but her two hands caress the panes.

SNOW: I call her into my world of deep frost.
ICEWOMAN: *Sighing.* I wish to lie out there, on that whiteness, face to face with the soft crystals.
SNOW: Her eyes glimmer when the moonlight touches them.

She tiptoes around the window and bends down to remove her two slippers on the other side. She pauses, breathing in the air, then begins to dance about the stage in ballet movements, turning cartwheels. After her dance, she removes her nightgown to reveal her pale-skinned body. She lowers herself on to the floor and lies on the stage, face down.

ICEWOMAN: The snow is cold but it does not numb me.
SNOW: I am icy and solid. All along her body, her knees, her thighs, her belly, her breasts I prick and hum her. I burn her, bring her to life.
ICEWOMAN: *Turns over.* My body hums.
SNOW: The light from the moon reflects off me and bathes her in light.
ICEWOMAN: Everything is black and white and silver.
SNOW: She is happy.
ICEWOMAN: This is who I am. This is what I want.

IV. Hugh helps Fiammarosa understand her element (and many other things . . .)

Fiammarosa is draped in a sheer blue dress, her long hair flowing around her shoulders, facing Hugh, who is wrapped in a fur coat and sits at a desk with a large book open. The white lily is still present.

Hugh: Today, Fiammarosa, we are going to read the history of your ancestor.

Fiammarosa: Who?

Hugh: King Beriman, who made an expedition to the kingdoms beyond the mountains, in the North, and returned home with an icewoman.

Fiammarosa: Why?

Hugh: I'll show you. *He stands and moves around the desk, taking Fiammarosa by the arm and bringing her to the window.* Look at the snow on the lawn, in the rose-garden.

Fiammarosa blushes and brings her hands to her cheeks.

Hugh: Yours?

Fiammarosa: *Nodding.* Have you been watching me?

Hugh: Yes, but only from the window, I swear. I was worried for you! . . . Do you not trust me? If I had followed you my tracks would be visible in the snow. But you do not see them, do you? Only yours — fine, elegant, naked.

Fiammarosa: I suppose.

Hugh: I have been watching you since you were a little girl, and I recognize happiness and health when I see them.

FIAMMAROSA: But why? Oh, tell me about the Icewoman, Hugh!

HUGH: *Walking the stage.* She was wondrously fair and slender, so the King loved her distractedly, but she did not return his love. Her father gave her to him as a pledge for a truce but she was stubborn and refused to learn the King's language. Sometimes she was seen dancing naked by moonlight on the longest night of the year with three white hares. Later, she gave birth to a son, who was eventually taken from her because the priests thought she was a witch. They threatened to punish her by burning.

FIAMMAROSA: What happened?

HUGH: The man who loved her would not allow it. Then one day, three Northmen rode on white horses with axes in their hands, up to the castle gate, and demanded the Icewoman back. She was fetched out, and one of the Northmen mounted her behind him. They turned and rode away together.

FIAMMAROSA: And?

HUGH: The Icewoman did not look back. The King died soon after, and his brother reigned until Leonin was crowned.

FIAMMAROSA: Leonin?

HUGH: Leonin was the son. He was warm-blooded through and through – the ice of his maternal stock was melted away to nothing.

FIAMMAROSA: Really, Hugh?

HUGH: Yes, and I believe that after generations, a lost being can find a form again.

Pause.

FIAMMAROSA: You think I am an icewoman.

HUGH: I think she is part of you and so I worry.

FIAMMAROSA: I felt a chill in my bones, listening to your story.

HUGH: *Approaching her, face to face.* It is *your* story, Fiammarosa. You too are framed for cold. You thrive on it. *Pauses.* I must help you! We must build icehouses in the palace gardens that can protect you.

FIAMMAROSA: You understand me, Hugh. Out there in the snow, I am alive. In my childhood, I always felt stifled ...

HUGH: I know. *He takes her arm affectionately.*

FIAMMAROSA: You choose your words very tactfully. You said I was 'framed for cold', but you did not tell me I had a cold nature. The Icewoman did not look back at her husband and son. Was she cold in her soul, as well as her veins?

HUGH: You tell me. Perhaps she saw the man as her captor and conqueror. Perhaps she loved someone else, in the North. Perhaps she felt as you feel on a summer's day, barely there, moving in shadows.

FIAMMAROSA: How do you know how I feel?

HUGH: *Leaning to her.* I watch you. I study you. I love you.

Fiammarosa averts her gaze and turns her body away.

V. The King summons the Princess for a chat

The stage is bare. The King is sitting in a chair as the Princess approaches with a respectful bow.

KING: Hello, my Princess.

PRINCESS: Hello, King. You summoned me?

KING: Yes, Princess. How old are you now?

PRINCESS: I am sixteen, King.

KING: You are a woman, then. Princesses are expected to marry, and you, Princess, especially need a husband.

PRINCESS: But I am too happy alone to make a good bride.

KING: Nonsense. You need to be softened and opened to the world . . . So I have sent letters to the Icelands, to a respectable suitor, named Prince Boris, among many others. There will be many suitors, Princess, I have sent your photographs to many places.

PRINCESS: But King, I have a heart of ice!

KING: It is for your own good. You will see.

VI. The Princess, now at ripe-marrying age, meets Prince Boris from the Ice World and the tall, dark Prince Sasan from the desert

The white lily. Enter Fiammarosa and Prince Boris.

PRINCE BORIS: I am Prince Boris from the North.

FIAMMAROSA: Pleased to meet you.

PRINCE BORIS: Your father sent me your weaving and a painting of your white beauty. Thank you.

FIAMMAROSA: *Detached.* Thank you for your gifts, too. The silks, pearls, eggs and plates, the leopard, pony . . . what else? Oh, the music box — they're all very nice. But tell me about your kingdom.

PRINCE BORIS: I come from the North. It is cold and full of icebergs and glaciers.

PRINCE BORIS: *Handing her a necklace of bears' claws.* I want you to have this. It was worn by my mother, and her mother before her.

FIAMMAROSA: *Without taking the necklace, she places her hand on her throat.* I can't accept it. I am sorry.

PRINCE BORIS: But why not?

FIAMMAROSA: Goodbye, Prince Boris.

PRINCE BORIS: But . . . you would be the perfect wife for me!

The sunflower is present. Boris leaves and Prince Sasan enters.

PRINCE SASAN: *Bows then takes her hand.* Enchanted!

FIAMMAROSA: Delighted!

PRINCE SASAN: I was moved by your portrait. You are the woman I have seen in my dreams.

Fiammarosa smiles composedly. Sasan reveals a large gift sitting on the floor and wrapped in silk. She opens it to reveal what resembles a block of ice. She examines it, walking around all sides.

FIAMMAROSA: Why, I can look through and through! There is a glass palace within the ice, a castle! I can see the corridors and chambers, spirals and curves and curtained beds! *She caresses the ice.*

PRINCE SASAN: It is glass, not ice, but it is an image of my heart, my empty life, which awaits you, Princess.

FIAMMAROSA: *Stares at the block.* It is magnificent!

PRINCE SASAN: This is my world, a paradise with all seasons in one. I have come to ask you to be my wife, to come to my land of sand-dunes and sea-waves. Now I have seen you, I—

FIAMMAROSA: . . . What is it made of? It looks like frozen water.

PRINCE SASAN: I know, but it is really sand, melted and fused in a furnace of flames.

Their eyes meet and Fiammarosa trembles.

FIAMMAROSA: I did not know that glass was made from sand. Are you certain it's not ice?

PRINCE SASAN: I will show you more if you come with me to the desert.

FIAMMAROSA: Okay, Prince. I will come with you to the desert and learn about glassblowing.

VII. Hugh poses an important question to Fiammarosa (and many other things)

The white lily. Fiammarosa and Hugh face each other.

FIAMMAROSA: I am going to marry Prince Sasan, Hugh.

HUGH: I know, but only for his glass sculptures.

FIAMMAROSA: Would you prefer a necklace of bears' claws, if you were a woman?

HUGH: A man and his gifts are two things, and glass is not ice.

FIAMMAROSA: *Turns away, pensive.* Come with me, Hugh.

HUGH: I cannot, you know that. I belong here, where I am needed. But I am worried for you. How will you survive that hot climate?

FIAMMAROSA: Humans are adaptable.

HUGH: *Seizing both of her arms.* It's not so simple as that! Sasan will melt you into a puddle!

FIAMMAROSA: Love changes people. If I use my willpower, I shall be able to live. I would die living without the man I love . . .

HUGH: *Stepping back.* Can people like you and Sasan, who thrive in two opposite worlds, live happily together?*

FIAMMAROSA: *Shaking her head.* I don't know, Hugh.

---

* 'Are we to suppose that because all things are composed of fire and water – those two discordant deities – therefore our father did conjoin these elements and thought meet to touch the body with fire and sprinkled water?' – Ovid, *Fasti*, Book IV.

VIII. Fiammarosa and Prince Sasan discover
their differences

In the darkness . . . A woman's scream.

Prince Sasan: What is it?

Fiammarosa: *Sighing.* . . . Oh my love.

Prince Sasan: I have hurt you. Look! Your skin is red
with burns!

Fiammarosa: No, no, they are marks of pure pleasure. I
shall cover them up, for only we should see our happiness.

*Lights. The lovers lie entwined in a bed draped in red velvet. Nearby
is a vase with sunflowers.*

Prince Sasan: You are ice and I am fire.

Fiammarosa: So how do we survive?

Prince Sasan: I don't know, my Princess. *He holds her in
his arms.* Ice is most beautiful when lit up by flames, and
fire is most beautiful reflected in the ice.

Fiammarosa: Yes, Prince, but when drawn together the
flames melt the ice creating water that, in turn, drowns
the flames. Out of mutual beauty grows mutual destruction.

Prince Sasan: Shhh . . . I will make you a palace built of
glass in the mountains, with air, light and water, something both of us can live in!

They begin to kiss. Lights off.

IX. FIAMMAROSA AND HUGH'S LETTERS CROSS PATHS IN THE POST (UNLUCKILY)

Holding letters in their hands and facing the audience . . .

FIAMMAROSA: I am dying a little daily, dear Hugh. I am not well and growing weaker.

HUGH: I am so happy, and though far away, I hope you will share my joy. I have married Hortense, the chamberlain's daughter!

FIAMMAROSA: I believe I am with child. I am afraid, being in a strange place with strange people. I am terribly alone and sick in this strange land!

HUGH: I am contented in my new house with my wife who loves me, my good chair and sprouting garden.

FIAMMAROSA: The molten heat outside oppresses me. The days are long, as you said they would be.

HUGH: Although I shall never be quite contented. When I saw you dance on the untrodden snow, in perfect beauty, the possibility of my settling into this life was taken away.

FIAMMAROSA: Sasan leaves me and goes away on long journeys. I need your cool head, Hugh, your wisdom. I need our conversations about history and science, your counsel, familiar voice, and good sense.

HUGH: I can't live in any of your worlds, Fiammarosa, not at the extremes of experience, as you can. I see now that extreme desires extreme, and that beings of pure fire and pure ice may know delights ordinary people must glimpse and forgo.*

FIAMMAROSA: 'Could you at least come to visit?

HUGH: Be happy in your way, and remember me, when you can, who would be quite happy in his way if he had never seen you.

The lights dim.

X. THE STRONG FATHER AND THE EXHAUSTED MOTHER RECOGNIZE THEIR EVENTUALITIES

Darkness, then a woman's scream.

FATHER: What is it?

Lights. A sunflower surrounded by white lilies is sitting on a small table behind the Mother and Father, who interlock hands, each holding a baby, gazing downward.

MOTHER: Twins!

FATHER: The boy resembles his mother, pale and golden.

MOTHER: The girl resembles her father, a glassblower's mouth.

FATHER: *Turning to his wife.* There is no fault in them.

---

* The problem of opposites called up by the shadow plays the decisive role in alchemy, since it leads in the ultimate phase to the union of opposites, when two essential halves form the Whole, at the marriage of the King and Queen, according to Carl Jung.

MOTHER: Will they be safe here, with us, in this glass
palace?

FATHER: Yes, Princess. They can breathe and live in their
own way and you can too.

*Mother and Father freeze momentarily, and the babies are set
aside.*

MOTHER: Come dance with me, Prince, out in the snow.

Close curtain.

See HARMONY   *A. Hörnell, Sandnessjøen*

Further reading: Byatt, A. S., 'Cold', *Elementals: Stories of
Fire and Ice*, London, 1999.

❄

PRESERVATION. Which bodies will keep in the snow,
and which will not? In what condition is the body that is
preserved by snow? Is it shrunken or swelled or altered in
color or taste?

J. Dahmer, Wisconsin

❄

PROMISE

MAIA: You said you would accompany me up the mountain
and show me all the glories of the world.

Professor Rubek: No, I did not. What is wrong with you? Can't you see that the storm is approaching? Can't you hear the blasts of wind?

H. Ibsen, Oslo

❄

PSYCHE & COLOUR

I. PAIRS OF OPPOSITES = TWO POLES

BLACK	WHITE
DARK	LIGHT
DEATH	BIRTH
SIN	PERFECTION
CHAOS	ORDER
DESPAIR	HOPE
EVIL	DIVINITY
WARM	COLD

II. TWO MOVEMENTS

1. Resistance: a conflict of opposites which are united by a force driving the universe onwards

physical   ↔   spiritual

121

2. Inner/Outer

DARK	LIGHT
BLACK	WHITE
with hope	without possibility

III. ABSOLUTE SYMMETRY

millions of parts joining together in a definite form with endless inventiveness

See DREAM . . .   *W. Kandinsky, Berlin*

❅

QUIET, as snowfall muffles the world into stillness, and the flakes fall without sound. The wind is hushed. Looking out my window, I can hear words in my head, repeated faintly but boldly written in the snow that blankets my front stoop. I see these words, at the beginning of sunrise, "I just want to watch you." I imagine the stranger writing to me with gloved hands before I awoke, or perhaps the night before, stealthily outside my window foraging in the snow.

E. Nussbaumer, Amsterdam

REVELATION. I hold the scroll in my right hand, sealed with the seven seals,* and around me are the twenty-four elders sitting on twenty-four thrones, wearing white robes. In the middle of the throne are four living creatures that resemble, respectively, a lion, a bull, a man, an eagle. As I open the first four seals each of the creatures say, respectively, "Come." When I open the fifth seal I see the souls of the slaughtered. After the sixth seal there is a great earthquake and the stars fall down to Earth. With the seventh I announce the coming day of wrath, and we watch the heavens unroll. The creatures keep saying to me, "Fall over us."

YHWH, Omnipresent

✳

SCHMUTTER is a slang word used for garments or articles of attire, which can be worn to keep the body warm in winter, and may also serve as objects of preference in fetishism. This enthusiasm or worship, in obedience to sexual impulses, echoes a religious reverence for relics and holy objects. There are different forms of garment – or schmutter – fetishism, but in a large number of cases the isolated articles of apparel might be:

---

* Not to be confused with the 7 stages of the alchemical opus, 7 terraces of the ziggurat, 7 deadly sins, 7 planetary signs, 7 colurs of Buddha's staircase and 7 notches on a birch tree of the Siberian shaman.

The Boot or the Shoe, a covering for the foot. Such cases are numerous in which the boot or shoe, conceived as a means of humiliation, becomes an object of special attachment.

CASE 77. Minister, Z., aged fifty. His dreams at night were shoe-scenes: he stood at a shoe-shop window and regarded the elegant ladies' shoes or dropped at a lady's feet and licked her shoes. The sight and touch of a girl's boots had charm for Z., who confesses that nothing else in women interested him besides their footwear, not even bare toes. From time-to-time Z. would accost a prostitute and ask her to go to a shoe-shop with him, where he would buy her a nice pair of shoes; and demanded she walk in the street in manure and mud to soil them. Then Z. would lead her to a hotel and before entering, cast himself upon her feet and lick her shoes. After he cleaned the shoes in this manner, he paid her and went his way.

Fur, like Velvet, serves as a heat insulator and produces tactile sensations.

CASE 17. Mr I., aged thirty-seven, made the following statement: 'The furs have to be very thick and long and stand out to have effect. I am indifferent to coarse, bushy furs, porcupine, and also to seal, beaver or ermine. I similarly dislike hair that is overlong and lies down, like that of the grizzly bear. Yet, seeing a woman in furs or velvet, even better, wearing both, causes me vivid excitement. The touch of them overwhelms me completely! My greatest pleasure is to see and feel my fetish upon a woman's shoulder.'

A Handkerchief, tucked in the pocket, can be extracted for wiping the brow, blowing the nose, blotting the lips. It is the one article of attire which, outside of intimate association, is most frequently displayed and which, with its warmth from the person, who might otherwise be cold, may mistakenly fall into the hands of others.

CASE 187. A baker's assistant, Mr V., aged forty-two, arrested in August 1890 for stealing a lady's handkerchief; and when his house was later searched, 446 ladies' handkerchiefs were found. V. stated that he had already burned two bundles of them. Nothing else could be learned about him except that his father was subject to congestions and that his niece was an imbecile. It was proved that V. committed his crimes in obedience to an irresistible impulse.

The Night-cap, an article for covering the head and suggestive of undergarments.

CASE 37. L., aged thirty-seven, clerk, functions normal, was excited by the idea of an old, ugly woman's head in a night-cap. When he met anyone – man, woman or beast – with a night-cap on, he could not resist them. Either the cap or the head without the other object did not excite him.

See CRYSTALLISATION (NEGATIVE)

R. Krafft-Ebing, Berlin

SHROUD, a blanket, sometimes made of snow and covering the martyr, miraculously, St Eulalia, who is out-stretched in pure serenity, bare-breasted and half stripped of her robes, with a blonde swirl of hair spilling over the ground to accompany the fallen folds of her costume, one wrist rope-bound and resting on the stone paving in the forum; she, having fallen from the cross, is watched by the crowd: one man who shields his wife from seeing the corpse and two soldiers who protect the others with pointed spears; whilst nearby, white and blue birds peck at the snow around her, and one solitary dove rises, a departing soul.

See GALE   *J. W. Waterhouse, England*

❄

S
  L
    E
      D
        D
          I
            N
              G is going downhill with some sort of support under your rear end, i.e.: a sled, a sledge, a toboggan, a large tire, a piece of plastic or, for poor kids like me, a cardboard cut-out. When I was twelve my parents took me

sledding at Bond Lake, in Ransomville, fifteen miles outside of Buffalo, N.Y.; and I brought my cardboard cut-out.

Bond Lake had three hills: one kiddy, one amateur and one expert. My parents took me to the expert hill, because that's where all the other families would be, and the other families had teenage kids. The other kids had such fancy transports – with shiny blades to cut into the snow at rapid speed, big handles to clutch, gothic hood ornaments. *Dad! Why do I have to do this? I hate sledding!* I said, though he knew I was lying. I didn't want Dad to think I didn't like the cardboard sled he took all morning to make me, but I detested the thing! Cardboard gets wet, and then it gets wetter, and falls apart.

Drew Davidson came to my rescue, sixteen-year-old Drew with the shiny bald head (because he was playing the King of Siam in the Payne Street School Play), Drew with the wide smile. He offered me a ride with him on his black innertube, a big rubber donut; and I accepted. The snow smoothed all contours of the hill. It sloped down steeply, so at the top, where we mounted the innertube, we could not see the bottom. Colorful bodies whizzed away from me, some making straight tracks in the snow and others zigzagging the way down, until they were out of sight. I watched some sledders go for a running start and slam their bodies on to their sleds at take-off.

Drew looked at me and smiled. *Are you ready?* he asked. I must have looked scared. *One, two, three . . . Go!* He pushed off with his foot to send us downward; our arms around one another for support, bodies jostling, cold wind stinging our faces, we flew! Drew leaned to the right and left in a sad attempt at steering, and I followed suit, except there were so many people scattering on the hill, so many moving bodies. Still, we flew! Then I saw the entire ending in eighth notes . . . Closing my eyes before colliding with another sled holding four bodies, reopening my eyes and the flying leaves and people flailing their limbs in the air, tumbling like socks in the dryer, an elbow approaching my head at amazing speed. BAAAAAMM!

S. E. Miano, Buffalo, N.Y.

❄

SNOW: *Il cantar che nell'anima si sente.**

Petrarch, Vaucluse

❄

SNOW, unbroken white,
gently along the Yukon;
wolf-dog at my heels,
the Chilcoot Pass:
at forty-five degrees below zero

---

* The song one hears in the soul.

my beard and moustache freeze solid;
at fifty degrees below zero
my spittle crackles on the snow;
at fifty-five degrees below zero
my spittle crackles in the air;
at sixty degrees below zero
the creek freezes from top to bottom;
at seventy-five degrees below zero
the dog learns fire, wants fire.

See DRIFTING   *J. London, Yukon*

❅

SNOW, Lorenzo (b. April 3, 1814, Ohio – d. Oct. 10, 1901, Salt Lake City, Utah), fifth president of the Church of Jesus Christ of Ladder Day Saints, founded Brigham City, Utah, in 1853 and served in the territorial legislature from 1852–3. Incarcerated for polygyny in 1856.

Who's Who in America

❅

STREAMERS:

At 11 o'clock that day the sun's rays broke through the clouds like gangbusters and never let up. I set out for a bike ride with my best friend Louise, who lived across town, had raspberry-glossed lips and smelled like cider and cinnamon, even in the summer.

Side-by-side, we raced down Broad Street, a narrow lane that forced us to squeeze together and bypass parked cars or trash cans. No better place to be. The pavement, freshly tarred, spread before us like a thick black carpet and glistened in the sun. The world was asleep: only the Popovichs and the Yunkhes were awake before noon on a Sunday, but they were over sixty so they didn't count. I loved it, and at nine years old, summer was the kind of time I could fill my days with only the things I loved – like lemonade, hammocks, katydids and, of course, bike rides. The beginning of winter was miles away.

Louise popped a wheelie, teasing me with her new Schwinn, a bracing silver princess that made my rubber Huffy look terrible. Sure, I was proud of my matching pink-and-green streamers, but Louise's had a water bottle and a place to stash peanut butter and banana sandwiches. I was so jealous! When we free-rode down the Broad Street hill, Louise covered her whole face with a smile. She was a vision of perfection: brown hair curled under with precision, hazel owl-like eyes and a nose full of freckles. Then she stuck her tongue out and threatened to jam a stick into my spokes . . . As if.

Suddenly, there was a loud clanging.

We were not alone.

Puutttttrrrrrrrrrrrr . . . It was coming from Maplewood

Park. As the sound grew closer I spotted a fast-moving vehicle emerging from between two big maples. Puttttttt-tttttrrrrrrrrrrrrrrrrrrrrrrrrrrrrrrrrrrrrrrrrrrrrrrr . . .

"Hey, is that 'Crazy Eddie'?" Louise shouted. She meant the guy who hit our neighborhood once a week for leftovers from the trash.

"Yepper!" I yelled. What was left of Eddie's hair stuck up on end and made him easy to spot. "Slow down!"

As we pulled our brake handles to slow into a more controlled cruise, Eddie looped toward us on his moped, staring down at his feet while he pedaled. His back basket was full with soda cans, old socks, plastic containers and plywood.

Louise shouted, "Honk your horn! Honk your horn, Eddie!" (Though it was early morning, it was okay to yell this to Eddie at anytime, under any circumstances, at least in our neighborhood. So if we hadn't called out, we'd have disappointed not only Eddie, but everyone else too.)

Eddie honked his red horn and looked up at us with saliva darting from his agape grin: middle-aged, he still had zits.

"Yeeehawww!" I yelled.

Louise wouldn't quit. "Do it again, Eddie! Do it again!"

Eddie bounced and jiggled, up and down, up and down on his seat, not paying attention to where he was going, as he honked his red horn again and again. He veered closer and closer to our territory. Louise pedaled on the outside, hedging me in. The curb loomed.

Laughing, she yelled again, "Honk your horn, Eddie!"

Incidentally, I smashed into the Yunkhes' white picket fence.

Then I flipped over the handlebars, and landed on my head in the lilacs, on my back in the mud.

Louise was still laughing.

Mr. Yunkhe peered out from his butterfly bush and ambled over to scoop me up with one strong arm, the other hand clutching a hoe. My eyes fluttered and gazed above at his suntanned face and greased salt-and-pepper hair. I'd seen him many times before as I rode by his house, when he'd wave or give me candy, but never so close. He was a tall, handsome man, with silvery hair, a slight moustache and ocean blue eyes. He smelled of Brussels sprouts, my favorite vegetable, and Old Spice, the aftershave Pop wore. He held me gently as he carried me toward the house. I could see Louise's feet trailing behind as I peeked around Mr. Yunkhe's shoulder. I also spotted my bike with its twisted front wheel jammed between the fence pickets. My bike chain, uncoiled, dangled from the oily gears.

"Thank you for . . ." I began.

"Oh, no problem," he said. "I was wondering when you'd come visit me. It's too bad you're hurt, though."

Soon we were inside the cottage, and Mr. Yunkhe laid me down on a corduroy divan. He sat on the floor, put a hand to my forehead and looked me over.

"You look like your mother," he said with a slight accent. "A real beauty."

I smiled. My eyes brightened. "Thank you."

"Beautiful blue eyes," he remarked.

I blushed. "Your eyes are blue too," I said.

Mr. Yunkhe smiled. "Are you Polish?" he asked. "I'm Polish."

"Half," I replied. "Polish and Italian."

"Band-Aids, for your pretty little legs," he said as he rose and went to get them.

My shins were stinging. I closed my eyes and told myself to keep breathing. But when I reopened them, everything was out of balance. I recognized Louise's outline; she sat near my feet, smiling. Curiously, I surveyed the room. It wasn't half as pretty as the garden outside. It looked like a farmhouse that I once visited near Canandaigua with its stiff furniture and wicker. The walls were beige. There was a cherry staircase, an endless succession of corners leading to various rooms, and tables holding photographs of young girls, whom I assumed were the Yunkhes' children. I also assumed they were now grown, and lived far, far away. There wasn't so much as a piece of art, a radio or a TV. The only visible door was a swinging one into the kitchen. An older woman, whom I'd never met before, sat in a wingback chair near the fireplace wearing a housedress and a friendly face.

"Are you all right, sweetie?" the woman asked, her words pouring out like molasses. And her chin wobbled when she spoke.

I nodded.

"Mr. Yunkhe will take good care of you, don't worry," she assured. "You're the Salerno girl, aren't you?"

I nodded again.

"Her name's Stella, Mrs. Yunkhe," Louise piped in.

"Oh, wonderful!"

The pain pounded inside me like a steady heartbeat. I suddenly felt very sad, mostly because I hated strange places and wanted to go home. *Where's Mr. Yunkhe? Just hurry!* I drew in one big breath and then slowly, unexpectedly, tears poured down my cheeks, dripping off my chin and on to my shirt. Louise lifted my feet to her lap and began to stroke my legs with her soft hands in a slow, comforting motion.

For a fleeting moment I could smell her cinnamon.

"I'll get some cookies and milk," Mrs. Yunkhe said. "Louise, dear, do you mind helping me in the kitchen?"

Louise hesitated and stared at Mrs. Yunkhe with her lips pressed tightly together. She looked as if she had swallowed some vinegar. "Um, I think I should stay with Stella."

"Oh, come on, sweetie," Mrs. Yunkhe coaxed. "It will only take a few minutes. Besides, you haven't come to visit me lately and you remind me so much of my girls when they were little."

I wanted Louise to stay with me, and I tried to tell her but only managed to groan. She turned to me and whispered, "I'll be right back."

Mr. Yunkhe descended the stairs with a tin of Band-Aids.

"Oh, good," Mrs. Yunkhe said. "Just wonderful."

He ignored her.

Louise slipped my feet off her lap and rose up, grabbing the patchwork quilt off the back of the couch to drape over me. As she followed Mrs. Yunkhe toward the kitchen, she looked back at me, eyes like two big olives without the pimentos. The pantry door swung shut and rocked a little. Then it seemed I spent the whole day alone with Mr. Yunkhe, but the bell-shaped wooden clock resting on the mantel read five-minutes-after-seven the whole time.

He leaned over me, pulled the quilt down and placed his clammy hands on my belly. I thought he might've been a doctor because Dr. Szirmai always did that during my check-ups and Mr. Yunkhe seemed to know what he was doing. So I closed my eyes like I did at the doctor's office. I let my stomach and shoulders and legs relax. His hands moved over my stomach in a circular motion, which tickled, but I thought I should keep still. Then his hands moved from my stomach, down, down, below my belly button. My body tensed and I opened my eyes.

"What . . . What are you doing, Mr. Yunkhe?"

"Just relax, honey. Keep still. Close your eyes."

I wiggled my legs. "But . . ."

"I won't hurt you, just close your eyes."

Why am I so nervous? I wondered as I closed my eyes. *Trust him.*

He leaned over me, so close that I stopped smelling the

good earth and was consumed by a musty, rotten odor. Suddenly, my body jerked as Mr. Yunkhe yanked my Bermuda shorts and cotton underpants down to my knees. My legs quivered so much that the patchwork quilt slipped off my feet to the floor. I opened my eyes to see Mr. Yunkhe pulling his pants down. I wasn't sure what he was doing, but I wanted to reach and pull up my flowery-print panties, to run away. My body wouldn't let me. It was anchored to the couch. I stared past the living room, into the dining room, at the pantry door, waiting for Louise to return. I gathered enough strength to sit up, but when I did, he forced me back down with two hands and lowered himself on to me. His calloused hands chafed me between my legs as he kissed my stomach. He reached up and touched my nipples and pressed against me, between my thighs, breathing heavily and grunting. My whole body burned. Keeping my eyes closed, I tilted my head to the side for some air, and a throbbing ran all the way from my lower body to my heart. *Maybe he'll stop. Maybe they'll come back out. Maybe I've been too nice to him or maybe this isn't really happening . . .*

My soul became a balloon that floated unbounded and traveled into a timeless world. Below, I could hear the old man clearing his throat, but above, in the floating world, I swept through a cloud filled with thunder. Below, a bead of sweat fell from the old man's forehead on to my chest. Above, I broke through a spatter of rain into the sunshine.

Suddenly he stopped and collapsed near my feet, half-on

and half-off, and I felt Mr. Yunkhe's whistling breaths on my legs. I wondered if he might be dying, but then I thought: no, he's just old. A minute passed and Mr. Yunkhe moved away from me. My eyes fought the stale dew and zeroed in on the pantry door, waiting.

I reclaimed my wandering soul.

As Mr. Yunkhe reassembled himself I reached down for my clothes. He pulled up his pants and wiped his damp face with a handkerchief then helped me pull up my shorts. As he was doing so, I looked down at myself and noticed two small dirt marks smudged near my hips: a gardener's fingerprints. He rearranged my shirt so it covered my belly. Then he applied two Band-Aids to my scuffed shins. Soon, the quilt was tucked neatly around me and he propped up my head with a small pillow.

Mr. Yunkhe stepped back.

"It's okay, honey. You're becoming a woman now, and this is just something adults do. It's normal. Don't worry, okay?"

I nodded, my face flushed and embarrassment crept up to my earlobes. I felt different, but I wasn't sure how or why. I felt sick.

He didn't look into my eyes. "Just don't tell anyone, though. Other people might not understand."

I nodded again. *I don't want to tell. Who would I tell?*

"Stella, this is a special secret between you and I. Don't ever forget, okay?" Mr. Yunkhe said softly, winking his blue eyes.

"Okay," I whispered. After all, we did share something special, something I'd never known before. More than just lollipops and smiles, it was the little secret that brought us close together. Mostly, I just wanted everything to go back to the way it was before.

And it did, at least I thought so.

The room was transformed into a normal-looking living room again. The Yunkhes were a kind, happy old couple. Mr. Yunkhe was only the man who rescued me from my fall, who waved to me and took care of me.

Louise came through the pantry door with a fake gap-toothed smile on her face. Mrs. Yunkhe followed with a tray of cookies and milk.

I could almost smile.

"We had to frost some cookies, so it took us longer than we expected," the old woman said, blinking with every syllable.

"Yeah, and I showed her where my tooth fell out," said Louise.

Mr. Yunkhe headed up the staircase. He ascended while adjusting here and there, hiking up his worn and faded jeans. He didn't look back, but for some reason I wanted him to.*

"I wanna go home," I said, getting up from the couch. My

---

* The alchemical imagination is present in the mind aware of its own division, for the Work involves the theatrical representation of an intimate discord.

legs almost gave out, but I knew it wasn't because of my fall in the garden.

"What about the cookies, dear? We did all that hard work."

"I'm sorry, Mrs. Yunkhe, but my parents are waiting."

"Oh, that's okay. I suppose you're hurting too."

"Yeah," I said. *Like I'm going to die.*

Louise grabbed a cookie. "Thanks, Mrs. Yunkhe."

"Well, it was certainly nice *having you*," Mrs. Yunkhe said.

As we walked out the front door, I took one last peek inside and all I could see was the empty couch. Even the patchwork quilt was gone.

Outside again, the sunshine afternoon soothed us with its buzz of sprinklers, picnics, potato salads and playthings littering the lawns. Suddenly I hated it all; and as Louise and I began wheeling our bikes back to our houses, I was praying for winter. I wondered if Louise had ever done anything like that with Mr. Yunkhe, and wanted to ask her, but I was too embarrassed. After a long awkward silence, Louise finally spoke.

"Sorry you got hurt," she said.

"I'm okay."

"You sure?"

"Yeah." *I'll be fine. I'm a big girl now.*

As we reached my driveway, Louise stopped and turned to me. She had a mouth full of marbles. "I . . . I," she stammered. "I hope . . . uh, Pop can fix your bike."

"Me too," I said.

"I hope you feel better."

"Me too," I said, "but I think it will take awhile. At least until winter."

"What?"

"Oh, nothing," I said, and turned my crooked bike into the driveway. The chain scraped against the ground as I made my way to the garage. I leaned the Huffy against the cement wall, and noticed only a remnant of my pink and green streamers left on my handlebars.

See FIBS OF VISION   **S. Sansone, Boston, Mass.**

❇

ЖУРА́НИЕ — n. A ripple, a murmur. The family of Windeck lived in a castle at Neu Windeck, but their race had declined steadily so only the Count and his daughter were left. Adelheid of Windeck was a haughty and stubborn woman. One day she scorned a young man of nobility, to whom she was betrothed, and later watched from her window as he jumped into the cold water and disappeared beneath the ripples of Lake Constance.

Therefore, the mother of the youth cursed her, saying; 'Adelheid of Windeck, from this day forward you shall never experience love, neither in living nor in dying. Until you are wooed by a lover as pure as my son, whom you drove to suicide, you will never be at peace.'

Adelheid laughed. 'Begone, old witch,' she said.

However, years passed and the lady did not marry. Eventually Adelheid died and was buried in the family tomb.

The people of the neighbourhood claimed they saw strange lights flickering through the castle's turret windows, floating from room to room like dancing ghosts. Wayfarers observed a woman in white with long auburn hair walking around the walls. Peasants themselves heard her murmurs.

One day a huntsman chased a deer into the courtyard of the castle, but considering he had journeyed a long while, gave up the chase and reclined on the grass. He closed his eyes and drifted into a deep slumber, the most peaceful he'd had in ages.

Soon it seemed he was in a stately dining hall surrounded by marble statues. In the centre of the hall he saw a table set for two, richly laden with all manner of dishes and decked with gold and silver. A door opened and a beautiful maiden appeared, adorned in white, with flowing locks of fair hair and the most resplendent jewels; and it seemed to him that he had never beheld a woman so lovely.

The woman took the huntsman's hand. 'You must sup with me,' she said.

'Yes, fair maiden,' the huntsman replied as he sat down. He gazed at the woman who filled his glass with wine.

'I am the last of my race,' she said. 'My father and brothers are dead.'

The huntsman's heart ached to think that she lived all alone in the enormous castle. 'Marry me then,' he said. 'I'll take care of you forever.'

'Sir Knight, do you really mean that? Are you prepared to wed me here and now?'

He fell at her feet. 'Yes, maiden. I wish nothing more than to be with you to the end of my life.'

The woman rose and went into another room, returning a moment later with a bridal veil covering her face. 'I will marry you. But the ceremony must take place immediately.'

The huntsman was willing, so he took the woman's outstretched hand. She led him through a door across the hall, through many stone passages and dimly lit hallways to the chapel.

The woman stood at the altar while the huntsman observed stone figures of bishops, knights, priests and cavaliers like ice sculptures all around. He shuddered.

Suddenly — he could scarcely believe it — one of the white figures was coming to life! A bishop, dressed in regal robes, stepped down from its pedestal and advanced in front of them.

The bishop faced them with a prayer-book in hand. 'Curt von Stein, wilt thou take this maiden to be thy wedded wife?'

The huntsman could not speak. Then the other statues also came to life, and formed a procession behind them.

'Curt von Stein, wilt thou take this maiden?'

The huntsman looked at his bride. Lo and behold, she wore the hue of death! All the colour and beauty had vanished from her; she appeared as a corpse. He was overcome with alarm and fell at the altar, covering the feet of the woman like a shroud.

Later that night the cold awakened him. He was lying on the grass in the courtyard underneath a full moon. He rose quickly, mounted his horse and rode off. But on leaving the castle precincts he looked back, hearing ripples of what seemed like a woman's murmur.

See DARKNESS   ***Griselda of H., Black Forest***

❄

TESTIMONY

Let me tell you the one true snow story, though not the one you would expect from someone who has spent most of his adult life poring over 'idiotically symmetrical crystallometry'— rather, a more important one, about her, for her, to her —

To *you*, my devoted apprentice, my favourite poet, my white butterfly, who is every woman in these pages, but the one great woman in my life.

Do you remember the Crimea and that particularly severe winter years ago, when the entire city was smothered in snow? I recall the whirling nothingness as I walked

through the park in Livadia that day — listening to the
primeval hush — and entered the unknown. Amidst the
swimming snowflakes I gradually made out the form of
a woman who sat on a bench near the path that led to
Oreanda. Flakes zigzagged through the sky and settled on
her cheeks and eyelashes, melting there. She looked about
sixteen years old, but drawing closer she seemed older,
almost like a gazelle in woman's form. I wished to speak
to her immediately. As I mustered up the courage and
advanced towards the bench, her voice rang out and broke
the silence. I stopped in my place, so as not to disturb the
songstress and rob myself of this pleasure. She began a most
delicious tune that Pushkin was fond of —

'Over the plains so broad and white
The snow our bitter tears hath buried'

As her voice swept through the wind to reach my aston-
ished ears, there came upon me an inexpressible feeling for
the world, a gratitude that broke out of my soul. The notes
flew through the air like angels 'wearing the snow-white
plumage of delight', and I thought; she is truly fragile. *To
love and to kiss her must be divinely beautiful.* Simply listening
to the woman was like dying from too delicate a delight, an
overwhelming joy that rendered me powerless; and for the
first time, the snow was anything but forgetful: *this memory
will be beautiful even in death.*

When she stopped and was quiet again, the wind whipped into my eyes; then she rose and walked towards me to pass by quickly and lightly, on her toes almost flitting, with an open book in her hand. I wanted to follow her,* but suddenly she turned around and gazed at me with ice-clear eyes, greenish-blue like the snow.

Extending her hand, she offered her book to me. I took it, and wrapping it in my arms for a long time looked at her – this member of a foreign species – so I can still visualize her there on the pathway in the wadded soundlessness of the snowfall. She smiled then;† and I realized that a woman who could either ruin my entire life or make me ecstatically happy had alighted upon me – that I must catch her and never let her go.

I understood immediately that I could love this woman to distraction; and thought these things, standing there, before looking down at the book she had given me, containing Bunin's poetry. As it was one of my favourites, I leafed through the pages swiftly, to find a particular verse:

---

* "In the people whom we love, there is, immanent, a certain dream which we cannot always clearly discern but which we pursue." – Marcel Proust.

Poetry = Existence = Love = Hope – Breton's formula.

† "What is a smile if not a flashing-out of the soul's delight, that is a light manifesting what is within?" – Dante Alighieri.

And there will fly into the room
A coloured butterfly in silk
To flutter, rustle and pit-pat
On the blue ceiling

I looked up from the passage, wetting my lips to speak, but I was alone. The woman had gone. Darling, that girl was you.

Did you know that I faithfully returned to the Crimea and that path where I saw her, where I saw you, darling, for a fleeting moment during that melancholy storm, and then lost you again? I waited a long time there, listening to the deathlike silence of the snow. Sometimes I would follow a woman who looked like you in some way, afraid to find it was not you, and to lose the feeling it gave me – always left with the fear and pain of being lost. Your absence seemed like an eternity. But God was kind to me: I found you, and everything began again.

Seven years later it is hard to believe I have never shared these things with you, perhaps I had not realized until now – no, no, accepted until now – that you have awakened me to a life that is not worth living without you in it. Rimbaud says that the only way an artist can discover the truth of life is by experiencing every form of love, suffering and madness. So, my darling, if this confession is not *too late* and you should want what is left of my life, it is all yours, of course.

I used to believe that an artist has complete meaning

alone; that one should begin and end his journey with only one set of eyes, acting as agent of his own transformation; that a companion is only a hindrance in his quest. How I was wrong! Two is better than one – for how will just *one* stay warm? – like Tennyson listening to the 'murmuring of innumerable bees', which, in winter, cluster together in the hive to generate heat. Thousands of bees in the centre gather enough warmth for themselves, but the ones on the outside shiver with cold as the temperature drops outside their home. In response, the ones in the centre flap their wings and kick their feet to stir up the others, until the agitation of the group spreads heat among the masses. I did not think the bees would return to me, especially not in order to teach me a most important lesson, but here they are again buzzing in my ear.

All this time I have been staring into the same hole, among the dead poets and artists, but not among the living. I believed that no other human being could understand or complete my meaning. Then the bees: *You need her*, they murmur, like everything else in nature needs something else; because art is the imitation of nature in her mode of operation, and everything exists as antimonies: Sun & Moon, Winter & Summer, Death & Life, Day & Night, Black & White, Ice & Fire. *You need her* because male and female, butterfly and moth, alchemist and poet are complementary parts of the same cyclical whole – meaningless without one another. It is the basic truth of alchemy:

things which may differ from one another in time, space, material, nature and many other characteristics *can possess and exhibit the same essential quality.*

For the sake of tradition, let me try to illustrate this for you:

It's called the Ouroboros, for its 'inharmonious harmony', and is supposed to look like a snake biting its own tail – the coming-together of two arcs into a perfect, eternal ring. (If you look closely at this drawing, you will recognize that *we* are the head and the tail, indissolubly linked.) When these antithetical parts join to become one, it is the achievement of the zenith, the perfecting of the hermaphrodite and the discovery of the *Materia Prima*.

My search for unity, zenith, enlightenment and stone, through the seven steps of the alchemical opus, has led me to *you*, my lapis and rebis.* All along I had been seeking the Grail everywhere outside myself, but because of you I have had *'une rêverie parlée'*, so to speak – allowing me to conquer the unconscious darkness that had been lurking

---

* The quest for a lost lover is analogous to the search for the Grail and the alchemical search for the lapis and rebis, or enlightenment.

within. Together, as male and female, butterfly and moth, alchemist and poet, I believe we can call forth the *anima mundi* or the awakening matter trapped in existence:

The Philosopher's Stone lies within our hearts.

Perhaps this is something you have already understood, and have been trying to reveal to me for a long time. Forgive me for trying your patience – you have so much wisdom for your few years! It reminds me of the time we were caught in a snowstorm after the fatiguing ascent of the Trettachspitze, which we'd heard was the perfect place for picking edelweiss. Do you remember? We slept soundly there, side-by-side, on our backs with the snow swirling down. You nudged me with your foot so I opened my eyes to the morning. It was colder than night, but snow was no longer falling. When I looked around, everything was fluctuating. Overhead, flying clouds; to the west, a large mound created by wind-swept snow; and everywhere east, deep white through the valley. I rubbed my hands, nearly frost-bitten. You were stretched out next to me – wool cap, collar, entire body was white. I looked at you looking away.

"Tell me," you said, "why you have been like a pool of frozen water since we came here . . ." I didn't reply, or move an inch, not even when the wind sent a new drift of snow over me. "Tell me," you said. "Otherwise how can I reach you?" After a moment you looked me in the eye, briefly, and I wanted to speak to you but my thoughts and feelings were trapped in a triad of cold, silence and height.

Instead, I began to fan my feet, knocking boots together – and remained silent, probably driving you mad. The snow cascaded from my legs as they formed two arcs in the snow. It was my only way to communicate to you, *with this movement,* so I began to spread my arms in a similar fashion; and fanned for a while, quiet, until you turned to me with your frosty face. I looked into your blue eyes until you understood and nodded, then mimicked my movements: fanning limbs, knocking boots, outspread hands – and the very ends of our fingertips grazing.

In many ways we are like the branches of a snowflake, working in harmony because each one knows what the other is doing; and it is a natural, spontaneous energy between us, resulting in what Rousseau described as *transparency,* a rare form of communication between two people that leads them into a state of total sentimental intimacy, *a merging with one another.* It is a language one hears in another's soul. There are other times, however, that our eyes play tricks on us. Perhaps you could not see all along that I was transparent – like the sea of cold on the moon, like polar bears and butterflies' wings, which appear white – and there I was opening all my inner parts to you. Perhaps I could not see all along that you were my happiness, because it was written white – and there you were with outstretched wings of hope to give me strength to reach you.

Well, here I am.

Please take this one confession in all its honesty – cleave

to it until we can meet again. I know you have resigned yourself to unhappiness, dear butterfly, after learning so early about suffering, but trust that I am coming for you immediately. And if I should not complete my journey, please have faith that our destiny is forever mutual. My wish is that you will take the key I have given you, which will allow you access to my entire life: my book of solutions, all the stories I have known. Take and do with them as you please. I trust you to fill in the blanks – with your stories, with ours – for you alone have full understanding of my soul. And then, before it is too long, you must come to me. Find me in our secret place – at the zenith, on the bridge made by the magpies intertwining their wings in the centre of the Milky Way.* I will meet you from the other side, disguised as Hikobushi, the bull driver, on the seventh day of the seventh month, you who are Tanabata, my weaver girl.

Until then, my days are frozen.

Compiler, Neuchâtel

Further reading: Walser, Robert, *The Walk*; Stifter, Adalbert, *Snow*; Hemingway, Ernest, *The Snows of Kilimanjaro*; Proust, Marcel, *Time Regained*.

---

* Gaia poured a sweet, white essence from her breasts, called White Snow, to create the galaxies. One such galaxy, the Milky Way, is "the winter street" which leads to heaven, according to the Swedes. To the Norse, it is "the path of ghosts."

TRUTH:

Keep me, O God. Show me favor for I have taken refuge in you.
Shay awoke with a prayer on his tongue – another morning
alone in his bed, another moment of purity in his life. He
stared through squinted lids out the window at the bare-
limbed smoke tree, bleeding and bending but staying erect
despite the driving snow. *Today is my special day*, he thought,
as he reflected on the past ten years – all blessed – which
included: first his dedication; second his baptism; third his
appointment to the ministry. Furthermore, when Shay
commenced his work he was about thirty-three years old,
being the son, as the opinion was:

> of Jesus,
> son of Joseph,
> son of David,
> son of Abraham,
> son of Noah,
> son of Adam,
> son of God.

Shay rose proudly and bathed peacefully, knowing he was
the prodigal son returned to his Father who, ten years
later, had finally digested the fattened calf. When he shaved
– carefully, meticulously – he felt all nine happinesses
fluttering down on him. He donned a tweed suit, blue tie
and wool overcoat so that, in one hour, everything about his
appearance was ideal: *streamlined* and *modest*. Shay stepped

out of the house and entered the streets of Buffalo, where the buildings rose like menacing stalagmites. He shuffled past them as he used to hurry past the West-Side drug houses on his way to grade school – head down, hands in pockets. Never once looking up.

Meanwhile Dora awoke, stretched her arms to the ceiling, then slipped off the quilt and planted her bare feet on the cold wooden floor. She sensed it wasn't the typical day, especially when she peered out the window and saw snow falling like long streamers released in celebration. She walked across the floor, avoiding piles of books and papers, and perched on the sill for a better view. Flurries blockaded her usual morning treat: university students riddled with smoke and laughter, trudging along Elmwood Strip, reluctantly on their way to morning classes. *They must be out there somewhere*, she thought, *hunched over in puffy jackets and braving the elements with surplus army boots. I can feel them.* Dora herself would not wear puffy jackets, at least not with surplus army boots, and especially not today. Still, her get-up was faithfully unpredictable – even for a self-help writer – a white T-shirt and lacy skirt topped with a white rabbit fur coat and cowboy boots that made her 5′ 10″ seem 6 feet. Furthermore, at thirty years of age, Dora was the daughter, as the opinion was:

of aromatherapy,
daughter of psychiatry,

daughter of I-Ching,
daughter of tinctures,
daughter of tobacco,
daughter of casual sex,
daughter of plastic surgery.

Staring in the mirror, cross-eyed, Dora hoped she hadn't put her lipstick on too dark. Then her eyes examined every aspect of her face; and she hated – no, *despised* – every bit of it, when in the mirror she saw *not herself*, but her mother, and her features one by one: pointed nose, possum's eyes, pasty complexion and poker-straight hair. Yes, she *despised* them, and wished them all away with her magic wand, one by one.

And I keep saying: "Oh that I had wings as a dove has!" On foot to the café, Shay headed down Elmwood Avenue and sensed something in the air besides snow fluttering down on him like a Bartók sonata. He wandered past the Albright-Knox Art Gallery, opened in 1905; Buffalo State College; Bailey Asylum; and off the main strip, where William McKinley's tombstone (he was shot during the Pan-American Exposition in 1901) sat unobtrusively in Forest Lawn cemetary. *What good news will I share today?* Shay wondered. *Will I share the story of Cain and Abel? Of David and Jonathan? Or is it a Naomi and Ruth kind of day?* When he arrived at the café, he ordered the usual: a double espresso and a bagel sandwich. He sat down at a table in the corner, facing the door, and pulled out his Bible. Shay turned to the book of Ruth, his favorite part, where she says to Naomi: "Do not plead with me to abandon you . . . for where you go I shall go, and where you spend the night I shall spend the night . . . Where you die I shall die, and there is where I shall be buried." Shay nodded to himself, moved by the intimacy of the words, and took a sip of espresso.

Opening the door, Dora called to her seven-year-old son Tom, who was stuck in the snow on the front stoop. "Come inside, Tom! It's freezing out there! . . . Oh . . . Don't move. Just wait there. I'll get you out." She'd just shoveled the stoop yesterday, and already sized up at least a foot of snow. It wouldn't let up. She dug Tom out with the red plastic shovel, which had been leaning against the house, then cleared their way as they walked to the car, lifting and dumping, shovelful by shovelful, until there was a small pathway leading from the front stoop to her car. When she pulled on the handle to open the door of her blue Volvo wagon, her hand slipped off. Damn. She dashed back inside for a bucket of hot water.

Jesus said, Feed my little sheep. Shay sunk his teeth into the cornmeal bagel packed with a delicious explosion of jalapeno, Cheddar and scrambled egg. It was one of the few delights he allowed himself, though he was far from being a glutton. Even the Lord allowed himself certain luxuries —

a bottle of wine, a fish or two. Christ once fed five thousand people in Bethsaida with his fish, starting with merely five loaves and two fishes. *Amazing*, Shay thought, *the perfect balance between survival and celebration.* He looked out the front window of the café and saw snowflakes coming toward him in great masses, masking his view of the street. He didn't know what he was looking for anyway.

As Dora pulled on to the Interstate highway, the brightness of the snow hit her windshield and jabbed at her eyes, which hadn't adjusted themselves after the long, black sleep. Soon she was able to steer using one hand, without too much swerving and squinting, and popped in a cassette of the Beatles' *White Album*. She twiddled her thumbs on the wheel. It was a mile to the school, and another few miles to the café, but as she entered the highway, she could hardly make out the yellow lines on the road, and her tires spun in the snow. The car pulled back and forth across the highway, following the grooves sometimes and other times spinning against the ice. Dora kept the car in control, knowing if she stepped on the brake or gas pedal she would slide; and whenever she hit a patch of ice she steered *into* the slide, not in the opposite direction. The speedometer read 15 mph and still she couldn't see in front of her as the snow came down heavier and heavier. She felt suffocated. *Why didn't they ever cancel school in Buffalo?* she wondered, and veered toward the exit for McKinley Elementary.

The children will gather around me, and I will guide them to the light. I hear their cries. Last August, Buffalo had thirty drug-related deaths in one month. Shay had been there, out in the world with its drive-by shootings, but everything was getting worse. Of course, that's why, since he put on a new personality according to God's will, the children were to him as lost sheep without a shepherd. Every time he attended evening worship they streamed over, in schools, to his chair, making his lap their haven. They gathered around him – chatting, laughing, embracing, pinching his cheeks. When he recognized a young one wandering astray, Shay came to the rescue with a heartfelt smile or a gentle touch and helped them cleanse their path. The congregation dubbed him, unofficially, "the father of the lost children." Otherwise, he was known as Brother Brown.

After Dora left Tom at school in the safe arms of Mrs. Presser (wearing her usual pink sweater and matching gym shoes), she re-entered the I-190, en route to her usual place for decent coffee before returning home to long hours of writing about sex. But as the car reached the highway, and Dora drove on, she realized the inevitability of her failure to withstand the horrific driving conditions of the blizzard. She could no longer abide by the rules because today there seemed to be no rules. This time, when she began to slide and steered in its direction, the tires spun and pulled the car further toward the shoulder of the road. This happened once, twice, and then it was all over: the car fishtailed and whizzed toward the guardrail and, as Dora braced herself, hit a gigantic snowbank with a thud. The engine roared. Dora was silent, stuck in a mound on the side of I-190, trapped inside a blue station wagon Volvo as the city rapidly became whiter and whiter. She took a deep breath. Then, hand on stick, reversed, forwarded and re-reversed in an attempt to rock the car out of its place; but the tires only kicked up masses of snow and, eventually, would not budge at all. She flashed her brights with optimism; *surely a plow will stop and dig me out*, she thought. And with the snowfall's slight transparency an occasional light drifted across her view, but the line on her gas gauge bobbed downward and, eventually, to the dreaded E. The heater purred quietly to a stop. As the cold leaked through the metal walls, the car windows frosted over quickly, so she had to work hard with leather gloves in clearing a space to see outside. It was a white-out. The stuff began falling merely three hours prior and already there were several feet on the ground.

They have wandered about as blind in the streets. Shay savored a sip of java and slipped on his spectacles to meet the day's headlines. More natural disasters, disease and war, more hypocrisy – all like Christ foretold, when in the last days, people would not have any natural affection, and with a *form of* Godly devotion that proved false to its power. When the people would live in darkness, without God's wonderful light. Shay recognized all these signs, and swallowed in the stuffiness of the café, wiping his forehead with a handker-chief. Unexpectedly, ten years ago, God's Word proved to be a lamp to his foot and a light to his roadway; one after-noon, Shay's hand stretched out his heart in prayer and found the Truth, which came knocking on his door *tap-tap*, just like that. Unexpectedly, Shay made love to his last woman. With heart-pounding resonance, the Truth sum-moned Shay *in all reasonableness*. He studied the Holy Word, from Adam to Michael to the Dragon at Har-Mageddon. He uncovered the falsities behind the hellfire and immortality of the soul doctrines; he decoded the prophecies in Revela-tion – from the Seven Bowls of Anger to the fall of Babylon the Great, the Empire of False Religion. Then he was sub-mersed in water in a pool of fresh water, surrounded by onlookers; and when he came up, the water rushed over him – his chest, neck, face – he surfaced and heard the applause of his new brothers and sisters. Shay was no longer a babe tossed about in the sea.

On every major radio station in Western New York, Mayor Masiello declared a State of Emergency and com-missioned a massive counter-offensive that would include road crews working all night to rescue the stranded. *I am a participant*, Dora thought, *in the November 20 lake-effect snowstorm that has Buffalo under siege, dumping enough snow to immobilize all cars in the entire city, either stuck in downtown gridlocks or highway ditches. Isn't that fantastic?* The last big one came in January 1977, when scores of pregnant women had to ride on the back of snowplows and tow trucks in labor and, later, would relate the story to the blizzard children they bore.

I kept on beholding in the visions of the night and see there! Flakes falling from the heavens, Shay thought, looking up and out the window, then back down to his good book, remembering the description of the One in the book of Daniel, the Ancient of Days, whose hair was like clean wool and clothing white just like snow. He turned to the passage and began reading: "His rulership . . . will not pass away, and his kingdom one that will not be brought to ruin." Shay's spirit was distressed, perhaps even frightened, but then he continued on: "The dream is reliable, and the interpretation of it is trustworthy." He prayed the Lord's Prayer: for God's Will to be done on earth as it is in heaven.

Buffalo was not always like this, of course. Sometimes it was a smooth ride down the I-190, alongside the lower Niagara River with its rushing beauty and the smell of chili hot dogs to guide her. *That's why I always return,* Dora told herself as if she'd forgotten, *for those days of release* – when suddenly the citizens of Buffalo break forth from their aluminum-siding houses and breathe the warm air; when the summer season ushers in sunshine, ladybugs and food fests sponsored by every known immigrant group. *Isn't that what we're all waiting for?* And Dora would tell herself every winter, usually in the seventh month, that she'd had many memorable summers during her thirty years in Buffalo. Whenever she thought about how a woman can run the entire term of her pregnancy completely surrounded by snow, like she had when Tom was growing inside her, she then recalled family picnics, boat rides and waterfalls. She remembered early days with Winslow, when she believed she was in love and ready to start a family, then after she married him, the profound disappointment over *the state of enclosure*. In living life, she thought, we fill the canvas of our existence. Each day, month and year adds brush strokes, lines, hues and patterns that define who we are and how we will be remembered. The differences in the way we complete our canvases account for the various ways in which we perceive reality. The temperature of the Volvo dropped rapidly and the prospect of someone stopping seemed unlikely, but Dora was content.

And you will know the truth, and the truth will set you free. Shay remembered the women he had loved and lost, in his reckless youth; he remembered cocaine nights and waking up in a stranger's arms: all those pleasures that still seemed attractive but mostly temporary, even working contrary to happiness. Shay lived his life on a teeter-totter, with the Lord on the other side, balancing him out day after day, motivating him to adjust himself and his spiritual weight. He'd come so far, but his transformation* happened naturally because, in truth, the Lord's load was light. Easy. Kindly. Like wings carrying him away. True freedom, without shackles of any sort.

Dora remembered the last day of her marriage. She'd had a signing at Borders for her new non-fiction book, *How to Spice Up Your Marriage in Five Minutes*; and later, found herself cleaning opened cans of green beans, moldy Emmental and oozing lettuce out of the fridge, still in her suit. She'd made sushi and then her husband of ten years, Winslow, came through the door with a new look. At twenty-nine her husband suddenly looked much older, with obviously dyed gray hair, a pair of reading glasses and unusually mature clothing. After dinner, while Winslow took a bath, Dora discovered an empty box of Viagra in Winslow's bedside table, and unearthed a woman's girdle, both stuffed under his tube socks. She confronted him while he was toweling off. He gave her a friendly kiss on the cheek and said, "I'm leaving you, Dora, for . . . for . . . uh . . . your mother." All

* "Look! You have taken delight in truthfulness itself in the inward parts; And in the secret self may you cause me to know sheer wisdom. May you purify me from sin with hyssop, that I may be clean; May you wash me, that I may become whiter even than snow." – King David's prayer for favor, after sinning with Bathsheba.

Dora could think to say was, "So whose Viagra is that? Yours or hers?"

Darkness itself will cover the earth. Shay stopped reading and looked up from his book. The lights had gone out in the café.

Dora began to cry when suddenly the floodlights on the highway sparked and went out, leaving her in darkness except for the gleaming light of snow.

* * *

My eyes have seen the glory. As everyone around him seemed to be in a panic, Shay noticed a bright figure sweeping through the snow outside and pausing, like Lot's wife, before it entered the coffeehouse. The angelic figure was shielded under a large fur coat, but when the instrument was doffed, was gloriously revealed like a Georgia O'Keeffe flower bursting from a slagheap. Still framed in the shadows of the entranceway, the figure radiated an aura of serenity and its movements were gracious and slow. Then, as if Shay was inside the Pantheon, a stream of fleeting sunlight broke through the above skylight, just like the "eye," illuminating the figure's face. Shay saw an angel before him, with ivory skin and lips dipped in cherry juice – the birth of Venus all over again.*

---

* "Pale were the sweet lips I saw, / Pale were the lips I kissed, and fair the form / I floated with, about that melancholy storm." – John Keats, *A Dream, after reading Dante's Episode of Paolo and Francesca.*

Quickly he bowed his head and secretly spoke to God with a psalm he'd said before, but never with such fervor. "You have taken up, dear God, the contests of my soul. You have repurchased my life. Myself I submit. Myself I commit." As Shay lifted his head, the figure extended a hand.

Dora wiped away the tears with her sleeve, then reached in the back seat for a wool blanket and wrapped it around her frame. I hope I am rescued soon, to see another Buffalo summer, Dora thought . . . She cleared the window another time. Outside, she saw a figure in front of her car, in the shadows, a dark figure standing there. She thought of locking the door, but waited with hand ready to punch down the button, as the figure approached. She could see that the figure was a man, smiling at her with a large set of white teeth, and instead of wanting to lock the door now, she was drawn to open it — yes, open it to a stranger, a mysterious dark figure which seemed to *beckon her*. She cracked open the door and peeked her head out. The man looked at her, standing a few feet away. Dora got out of the car and extended her hand.

Am I what you expected? — Shay and Dora asked each other simultaneously, at the right time and right place, during a blessed blizzard and an unfortunate power outage, amidst the sheer confusion that nature can cause, though all was quiet in Buffalo: a city which had, at that moment, achieved the perfect balance between black and white, blindness and revelation.*

Shay and Dora, Buffalo, N.Y.

❄

TULIPS. It is winter here and I am inside with the tulips.

S. Plath, London

❄

ULU:†

It's October and the autumn freeze-up, so we walk across the snow-covered tundra, towards the lake, our footsteps creating rhythms with the sounds of icy winds. We are on our way to reopen the old fishing holes because the ice in other spots is up to two metres thick. In our lake you can only catch char, but in the sea you can catch turbot, tom cod, polar cod, sculpin, ringed seal, bearded seal, hooded seal, harp seal, walrus, beluga, narwhal, bowhead whale and polar bear. We do not travel as far as the sea because my brothers and sisters are too young. So, days on end, I stand on the frozen lake with

---

* Phenomena are usually categorized in antithetical pairs, like day and night and the never-ending cycle of death and renewal.
† Rimbaud defines the letter U as "the wrinkled ease that alchemy imprints upon a scholar's brow."

my large family, waiting for char. Five of us stand around in a circle, perfectly still, holding our poles, while one of us – usually father – stands over the hole. Mother kneels on the ice. If not for the boots and slippers we wear, my family would not last in the subzero temperatures of the High Arctic, waiting for char. (Even at night our hairy footwear is invaluable, when they become toasty-warm pillows.)

If not for the kamiks that mother and I make . . .

You can tell if a skin will be good to work with just by looking: if the hair is curly under the neck it will usually be perfect for the kamiks. We store our skins – either seal or caribou – in the cold of the igloo, where they can soften properly. After they are cleaned, mother and I hang them out to dry. Once I choose a good piece, I mark the centre of it with my teeth, thread a rope through holes along the edge, gather it into a ball and stamp it for an hour until nice and soft. Then I lay the skin on the ground, hair side down, and place small stones around its edges. If it is caribou, mother taught me to soften it by chewing on it until damp and a lot easier to sew. To scrape, some lay it on the ground and kneel on its edges, but mother taught me to clamp it between my legs and pull it over my thighs. I hold the jagged edge of my ulu next to the skin, and, like slicing slivers of bread, start from the middle and scrape away from myself, removing all the fat and fascia. I do this procedure for several hours, until it stops crackling. The shaved skins will become soles that will hold up in damp weather.

We use our hands as a measuring tool to mark patterns for the soles, along with the vamps and leg sections of the kamiks. (If I am making a boot for someone else, it is helpful to examine their handspan or take an outline of their foot to get the right size.)

Next I fold the skin in half, flesh sides together, and the top piece overlapping the lower piece slightly, then bite along the fold in order to etch a pattern on one side. Using my ulu, I cut a sharp edge, which becomes a template for the other side. When sewing, I hold the point towards my palm and wind the thread around my hand, creating tension, then pull every third stitch tight as I move from right to left. Overcast stitches work well for the skins with hair, but for the shaved ones it is useful to vary the running stitch so the water won't leak through the holes. (Mother taught me that too.)

Vamps are cut with the grain of the hair travelling across the instep and sewn to the sole using a waterproof seam. I am careful to make the pleating even, so the boot will not twist. The leg section is attached to the vamp strip, and the sole is tacked to the leg section at the front, back and on both sides with blackened sinew. When finished, I rumple the seam gently to flatten it.

For decoration I use a piece of haired skin in a contrasting colour, and insert it into the leg section. Mother likes to use pompoms on the drawstring, while I stitch beads to the toes, which set them apart from the others, or appliqué bleached seal-skin figures on to the legs. On my own boots

ULU

I embroider one word: *okiutaqtuq*.* It may take me four days
to make a pair of kamiks, but I feel much better about them
if I take my time, even though I know the wearer will soon
grow out of them.

Bella Meeko, Igloolik

❄

UUKKARNIT, a West Greenlandic word signifying
'calved ice from the end of a glacier'. Eskimo languages are
polysynthetic, meaning that detailed ideas can be expressed
in one word, and many territorial differences are found in
word usage among the Eskimo, especially in defining snow.
Thus, the manner in which a Labradoran Inuit would denote
'bits of ice floating in water' would differ from the same
expression in Yupik. English has far fewer words to indicate
the solid form of water that crystallizes in the atmosphere
and, falling to the Earth, covers 23 per cent of the surface,
either permanently or temporarily, among them: snow,
sleet, hail, rain, ice.

Eskimos in W. Greenland use forty-nine words to
describe ice and snow, among them (besides *uukkarnit*):

I.   *Sinkursuim:* unstable slab of ice
II. *Masaaraq*: small ice floe not large enough to stand on

---

* "Having winter regularly."

III. *Piddilaq*: urine in the snow
IV. *Sullarniq*: snow blown in doorway
V. *Rigid ganaraq:* ice in hard form
VI. *Maniillat*: hummocked ice pressure ridges in pack ice
VII. *Reariswer itsat:* wolves copulating in the snow

from the notes of Rev. Julian Peck, Greenland

❋

VIRGINITY: Women in love, like Mary, walking home with me from the dance, both of us in ridiculous clothing me in a #3 football jersey and Mary in a long, loose-fitting bathrobe. How perfect it was, the two of us, trudging in the snow that burned our faces! I wanted to kiss her there under the streetlight, cherry cheeks and trembling lips, but she turned away from me, swinging her hair – looked back and smiled. I watched her sway down the street singing "Buffalo Gals," her voice ringing like silvery bells in the frozen air of twilight.* I wouldn't have remembered that moment if Clarence, my guardian angel, hadn't shown up . . . They promised him wings.

See NAKED   **G. Bailey, Pottersville,**
                          formerly known as Bedford Falls

---

* "'What do you want to speak to her for? She never speaks to anyone. She sings.'" – Heinrich Mann, *Professor Unrat* or *The Blue Angel*.

Further reading: Lawrence, D. H., *Women in Love*, England, 1920.

✳

WHIMSICAL. I am buried in a lonely churchyard on a hill in Oughterard. I can hear the snow falling faintly through the sky, covering the ground and shrouding my tombstone. I am not cold now, but I remember that night standing under a tree in the rain, and waiting for my beloved outside her house in Nuns' Island; the chill soaked me through and through. When I was in Galway and Gretta was great with me, her warm hand responded to mine. I sang to her "The Lass of Aughrim" as we walked in the country. But then she left me and I wanted to die.

M. Furey, Ireland

✳

WINK & WHISTLE:
Three days before Mom died I was the only one in her room.

I sat in a clumsy wooden chair next to her hospital bed, holding her hand and gabbing about nothing in particular – the June weather, the chewy macaroni served in the cafeteria, the flowers Pop had brought her, placed in a tiny vase on the windowsill. They were clipped peonies from our backyard. Their drifting fragrance somewhat disguised the ammonia and urine odor leaking into our small area, which was enclosed by a sheet-like curtain pulled loosely around her bed.

Pop and I were the only ones who knew it was cancer. It was our job to keep it secret so that my brothers and sisters, all seven of them, would not know the seriousness of Mom's illness and could huddle in the Guerriri family's protective shell, which somehow I imagined as a white bomb shelter. In school we did physical drills to learn how to survive: when the alarm sounds, cover your head, duck under the desk. *Duck and cover, duck and cover*, Mrs. Neal instructed. At home we learned emotional ones: sense confrontation, cover your true emotions, take refuge in the family unit: a place where the world's troubles and sorrows fade away. So when Mom passed I would be in charge of guarding the bomb shelter. Just seventeen in April, and already my duties were to get the children ready and on their way to Fletcher Street School every day. That, of course, and support Mom while Pop worked installing flash heaters.

Resting awkwardly on pillows the nurse had propped up for her, Mom's head looked large and mannequin-like. It was a huge bubble compared to her stick of a body. The hard edges of her bones poked up beneath the bed sheet, which spilled over her like a shroud. Her eyes were closed so I could see the tight wrinkles of her eyelids and the dark skin around them. I tried to remember the gaze of her sea-blue eyes, the way their shade defined her moods. They sparkled as two planetary stars when she looked at someone she adored. My brothers and sisters, who all had brown eyes, said I was lucky to have Mom's eyes but I wasn't so sure now. Mine seemed to be grey lately, despite my efforts to call up the blue – a dead giveaway for my anguish. I wanted to end Mom's pain. It nagged me worse than a sore tooth or a toe blister or anything else. Since Dr. Bilable told us she had two weeks, I thought of nothing else. Plenty of people's mothers lived to eighty; even seventy would be okay. Mom was only forty-two.

I hated my life.

Her breathing was quick and forced, like a person who'd just been pulled out of the ocean, rescued from drowning. I imagined her lying limply on the shore as I leaned toward the purple swell of her face. Then I brought my lips to hers, opening them with both hands, and breathed strongly into her mouth. She came up gasping and sputtering . . . if only.

When I concentrated hard enough I could make Mom appear as she'd been years ago – a woman with striking Czech features: the high cheekbones, widow's peak, a long narrow nose. I saw her in clips of random history; more recently as a woman with long golden hair, running up a hill in an A-line skirt as I trailed behind; earlier as a woman with cropped ashen hair bundled up in a faux fur, sitting in the snow on our front stoop; and when I was still crawling, as a woman with a bun of strawberry-blonde hair, her girlish body hugged by an apron as she made poppyseed roll. I see the photograph taken as she arrived at Ellis Island, pouting in Baba's arms with a scarf hugging her baby face.

And always there was Mom's magical wink and spirited laugh.

I have that laugh, the one that comes from Mom's side, the one that traveled from her mother – my Baba – to all of my aunts, to Mom, and then to me. It's alive and warm – slightly a cackle, slightly a giggle. When I was a child and couldn't fall asleep on stormy nights, Mom's late-night laugh used to travel up the stairs, waft into my bedroom and instantly calm me. The laughter was in stereo when my aunts visited on weekends. Aunt Anna and Aunt Milla would drive five hours from the Pennsylvania backwoods, stealing to our house in the "city" to instigate what I thought of as the apple-Danish-donuts-and-coffee exchanges, which could sometimes include quiche. Instantly, there was chatter. It was remarkable how, suddenly, Mom forgot her cereal-before-bedtime-at-10 p.m. ritual and stayed awake into the wee hours. I stayed awake as long as I could too, listening to all their stories. By far, Mom told the best ones. Her memory was an infallible microchip.

Along with the stories and the laughter, Mom winked magically like Rita Hayworth or any of the great bikini-clad beauties in 1940s pin-ups. But you had to remember the wink in freeze frame because no one ever hit the camera button fast enough to capture it. Not a normal closing of the

eyelid, but it was more like a twinkle, an enchanting bolt
of light. At times it came so quickly that you nearly missed
the moment, then waited anxiously for it again. And
when it came: a wink that could be simultaneously sly
and innocuous; sly because she knew she was being watched,
innocuous because the act blossomed from pure joy. Somehow Mom and her sisters had a way of maintaining balance,
even though they were constantly getting knocked about
like the red-n-white striped buoys I saw in the Niagara
River, which tried to stand up under the constant flow of
water coming from the great waterfalls upstream. And now
I was amongst them, sometimes wishing to sink under the
pressure as the smiles and winks gradually lost their luster.

A year ago Mom was fine: bouncing, laughing, talking.
She and Pop began to battle less, something god-like had
stifled their screams, and Pop came home from a seven-
month disappearance. I believed he'd fallen in love with
her again. I saw them together in the mornings, before I
left for school, sharing French toast and the early edition
of *The Buffalo News*. That summer we bought a farm out in
Lockport with sheep and an old shepherd to tend them.
Every Sunday, Mom and Pop would spend the entire day at
the farm. On occasion they took us with them and we
played volleyball, fusillading the white ball back-n-forth
over the net while they sat amidst the roses and talked. We
were finally a normal, happy family and I wished for that
happiness to go on forever. Then six months ago the same

god-like force stealthily let the air out of Mom and she deflated slowly, with constant headaches; all the time: sick, sick, tired.

I had an after-school job at Science Kit, a small factory in Buffalo that produced kits of beakers, vials and dissection tools to encourage elementary schoolers to become great scientists, though mad scientists was more like it. When I got home from work that Thursday six months ago, I was hungry for our ritual spaghetti and meatballs. I could almost taste the chilled mascarpone cheese blended with marsala in Mom's tiramisu. I removed my loafers outside, flicking them off to the side of the stoop so Pop and the boys wouldn't mindlessly trample them going in and out. After the door slammed behind me I took a deep whiff of the inside air. I had expected the aroma of stewing tomatoes, fresh basil and oregano, but all I smelled were the last fragments of pine-scented furniture spray and hints of bird crap; and Mom, who usually greeted me with an apron about her, did not peek at me from the kitchen. There was no spaghetti or meatballs on the table. The shades were drawn and the lights were off, except for the tiny light above the kitchen sink that cast my shadow on the living-room wall. The crossword puzzle sat undone on the coffee table in front of the striped orange couch. I closed my eyes briefly to savor the silence of tiny sounds: of the clock ticking upstairs, the boiler in the basement, the cars whizzing by outside. Within moments I was left with an urgent curiosity.

"Mom? Are you here, Mom?" I called out, and my voice bounced off the paisley wallpaper, up the walnut staircase and landing in the hallway upstairs.

I took the stairs two at a time and paused outside my parents' bedroom door. Only the creak of the boards sounded as I rocked there, back and forth. Their bedroom door was shut. It was usually open for us.

"Mom? It's me!"

Silence. I walked down the narrow hallway, sliding my finger across the flowery wallpaper. The black-and-white faces of Mom and Pop's European families, who immigrated to America just after the First War, looked at me sadly from their places on the wall and heightened the solitude. I reached my room, which I shared with Natalia and Stella and consisted of bunk beds, a chair, a desk and a closet crammed into a space equal to a prison cell. Mom and Pop knew how to save money: stuff all the children into one room and "*pasta e fagioli tutti giorne*" (pasta and beans every day). I put my backpack on the chair in front of our window already buried in clean clothes off the line. Pop, in an attempt to create a fire exit, had placed the chair there years ago. He wouldn't let us move it and had drilled us on fire procedures: First, smell smoke. Get up and wake up the others. Seal the underside of the door. Grab the chair and break the window. Use the chair to hoist yourself out the window. Shimmy down the gutter. Then help everyone else climb out.

Fortunately, we'd never had a fire in our Bouck Street

house. Unfortunately, the chair wouldn't help if we did. It provided an extra place to stow items like books, blouses and backpacks. And with three girls' laziness the room became smaller and smaller. Natalia and Stella expected everything to return miraculously to their proper places without lifting a finger. So if it did get tidy, the elusive cleaner was *me*, their older sister, trailing behind them with a trash bag and gloves. Otherwise, we wallowed in the mire. So, if there was a fire like Pop expected, we'd probably just use the stairs. It'd be better that way.

One of Pop's parakeets flew in and landed on my arm and I sneezed. Irritated I flung the bird away, so he drifted to a branch of the bird jungle gym that Pop had built on my dresser. He was one lone green parakeet in a team of six. Nat and Stella called them all by name but I couldn't care less. I pivoted and waited for more to follow, but the hall was empty. The year before, Pop had driven to Geneva to buy a male and female and eggs to breed them. I had to read the book on how to raise parakeets. I followed the instructions and then one day, all six eggs hatched. Now we had parakeets flying around crapping on everything. Mom screamed, Pop laughed and continued providing more sticks for landing places.

The telephone rang as I was undressing.

Margie.

My pleated skirt dropped to my ankles. *Hi Pop. What's going on?*

Could you take care of the kids when they get home? Pop asked.

Where are they? And where's Mom?

Listen, the kids are playing at the Mianos'. He paused. I could hear him breathing and although I couldn't see his face, I sensed that his left eye twitched as it did when he was nervous. *Call and tell 'em to come home for dinner. Andre is playing street hockey but he said he'd be home by six o'clock.*

A woman spoke softly in the background.

Where's Mom? I asked.

Pop said in a low whisper, *She's with me. We'll explain later, when we get home.*

Can I talk to her? I held my breath. *I don't know what to make for dinner.*

Find something — I've gotta go, Pop said hurriedly.

When will you. . . I began.

Click.

. . . be home? . . . Pop? Pop?

Pop's nine-month disappearance when I was fourteen was really a crack-up. He had a mistress, a younger woman whom I saw only once up close in the produce section of the Broadway market, gathering purple melanzane and massive funghi in her thin arms. She looked at me, moving on to the roma tomatoes. Then she smiled, but I looked away.

Using my toes I tossed my pleated skirt aside then pulled on a pair of khaki clamdiggers with a white blouse. After I phoned the Mianos' and told the kids to be home in half an hour, I searched the kitchen cabinets for something to make for dinner. The stuffed canned goods cabinet was stocked with chicken soup, green beans, creamed corn and water chestnuts. I knew those wouldn't go over well. The freezer held chicken and ground beef but I wasn't a food connoisseur. How do you prepare meat? Do you have to clean out the guts first? Remove bones? What's all that red stuff, blood? I knew how to make fried eggs, but not more than one at a time. I could scramble them, but how many to use? All of these questions were just too practical for me, someone who never watched Julia Child, and wished to console myself in front of my typewriter.

Wait.

Yes.

Perfect.

When the kids trampled in through the front door with their bags, binders and empty bellies, dinner was ready. On the dining room table sat eight bowls, eight spoons, a gallon of 2 per cent, and assorted boxes of cereal: Nabisco's Shredded Wheat (made right here in Niagara Falls at its first-ever factory), Life and Quaker Oats – a little something for everyone. Sitting at the head of the table, I chose the oats.

"We're having cereal for dinner?" Nat asked and I wondered if she, without a domestic bone in her body, could do any better. Whatever, she added, flipping her long dark hair and tossing her backpack on the couch. "I'll eat when Mom gets home," she told me as she headed for the stairs. I know she expected Mom to make her something later when she got home. At fourteen, she was so helpless. With my lack of practical skills, I couldn't blame her, really. But at least I had an excuse, a passion. She forfeited her domesticity for boys and bubble gum.

"Where's Mom?" Stella asked, slipping into the chair to my right.

"She's with Pop. They'll be home later," I answered, pouring the milk over my oats.

"Mmmm . . . Cereal!" yelled Isabella, running in circles around the table a few times until she settled in the spot to my left.

"Pass me the Life," Alex mumbled, plopping down into the chair at the foot and pushing back his curly brown hair, which hung loosely in his eyes.

Sam Jr. and Adam were wrestling in the living room. I could see Adam's arms flailing as Sam, the older of the two, held him in a headlock.

"Come-n-eat, guys!" I yelled. Sam laughed and Adam didn't answer; his face was turning red. "Let him go, Sam," I said. Adam squirmed and groaned. "Let him go for heaven's sake!" Soon enough, the two boys made their way to the dining room, but not before Adam got a couple of punches in on Sam.

I poured the milk into a bowl of Life. "How was school?" I asked Adam, hoping that he would tell me that today had been smooth-sailing, no kids taunting him in the playground, no scraps.

"Okay," he replied, "the same," an answer I didn't find comforting. At seven he was the youngest, and being smaller than most kids his age, he was the closest to Pop and the one Pop always protected. I think Adam hurt the most when Pop moved out of our house and moved in with the other woman.

We all knew Pop had been spending a lot of time with the neighbor (for surely a woman's boiler doesn't break down *that* often), a redheaded beautician named Fanny, everyone knew – from my boss to my classmates to Crazy Eddie, the neighborhood garbage picker. Everyone except Mom. Not until the two of them, Pop and Fanny, became mysteriously lost on the same day at the same time did Mom put the pieces together. She cried every single day for those months; I could hear her during the nights, her muffled crying.

Andre was home. I could hear him outside singing "Blue Suede Shoes." If Mom had heard him she would have given him a slap. She didn't like all that modern music. He came into the house with a bag that he emptied on to the couch: wrinkled sweats, socks, books, old candy wrappers and a pair of roller skates.

"Hi sis," Andre said. "Tough game. We lost." I watched him take off his pullover sweatshirt, laughing at his involuntary grimace as his sleeves trapped his Roman nose near his armpits. His usually silky straight black hair was a tangled mess.

"Pewwww!" he said while teasingly lifting up his right arm and threatening to stick his armpit in my face. "No girls for me, not smelling like this!"

"Gross . . . get away!" I yelled and pushed his arm away. At fifteen, Andre already towered over me: 5′ 10″ to my 5′ 5″. He was thin too, but not in an awkward kind of way; he was gracefully skinny like the Czech side. Andre was the kind of guy with creativity, charm, good looks, sensitivity and plain cool all rolled into one tight package.

At eight o'clock I coaxed the little ones into bed, read the next part of *The Wind in the Willows*, lightly tickled their arms and said prayers. On my way downstairs, I peeked into Andre's room and spied him painting his latest on canvas — a lovely squash and spectacles still life. I passed through the living room where Natalia sat on the rug, right in front of the television, wrapped in a patchwork quilt, sneaking her bowl of cereal and watching Ed Sullivan. Every minute the picture would flicker and fade, so she'd hit the top of the set to get it roaring again.

I stepped barefoot on to the cemented back porch and rested my arms on the wrought-iron railing that enclosed it. Spring had begun, taking the cool edge out of the evening air and leaving a fresh and earthy smell I loved. I could imagine the worms poking around in the grass, and in the garden where I planted my first strawberry patch at five years old. I found my usual quiet spot in a wicker chair on the back porch and rocked away, hoping to rock away the simplicity of my family and my routine. I looked out beyond our yard, beyond our back fence, suburbia, the earth and sensed a little bit of another, less troubling world where I was far more comfortable. I savored the pleasure of the red glow of sunset. Then I heard Pop's car pull into the gravel drive. Finally, when my eyes had fixated on one lone star, Mom came outside, letting the door close quietly so as not to wake the children.

"Margie," she said as she sat on the wicker couch. Mom's blonde hair was pulled back into a bun, but flyaway pieces were sticking out, and a couple strands in her eyes. Her face was blotchy and red, especially her nose, and her eyes looked stormy. "How'd everything go?" she asked.

"Fine," I answered. "But what happened?"

"Well," she said, sighing. "Pop took me to see Dr. Bilable today."

I looked at her profile; she was squinting in thought. Mom didn't believe in doctors, she never saw them.

"I went through a bunch of tests last week." Mom lowered her head and cupped her knees. "He thinks I have leukemia."

"What?" I gasped. "He thinks you have leukemia?"

She sniffled. "Well, he's pretty sure."

"No . . ." I said softly in surprise and, without looking at Mom, lifted my hands and covered my face. I breathed deeply for a while in silence and tried to think of something to say.

"Oh, Mom," I said. I couldn't comfort her, touch her, say

or do anything. I remained quiet in my chair, though stiffly, still rocking. I wanted to cry, but the tears stayed inside with all the other uncried tears of the last seventeen years.

Finally I reached out and rested my hand on hers. "It'll be okay."

She looked at me teary-eyed and my lips trembled.

I kept my hand on her arm, but her eyes moved away. She lifted her head and gazed intently at the sky, and maybe at the same lone star that captured me earlier. As I held her I wished for the disease to seep through her fingertips and spread into my veins, to transfer, so that she could go on living – and I, someone younger and less loved, could take the bullet for her.

* * *

It was still the first of three long days. From the hospital window, I watched a pack of teenagers riddled with snow, smoke and laughter move with the litter on the city street, probably headed for a heaping platter of hot Buffalo wings at the Anchor Bar. I thought about running out, joining them and taking a big piece of their freedom and youth – the things that were sucked out of me when Mom got sick. But I didn't go. The passing thought alone was disloyal.

"Margie, are you here?" Mom asked, just waking.

"Yeah, Mom, I'm still here," I said. Mom was still caged in her steel bed. "By the window."

Every few minutes I gazed out the window, waiting for the snow to stop, but it never did. It kept coming, and the leaves fluttered on to the window, carried by the wind off the river. Cars moved slowly along the street, spinning up snow. I watched the street life, bundled people bobbing below me, mad dashes for the entranceway. Then it would come: the lull between doctors or surgeons reporting to duty, the lull between families coming and going, when ominous shadows leaked in and perpetuated my loneliness. I was a single witness to the dark moments because they would quickly vanish with someone's heel hitting the pavement or someone cracking a smile . . . my little secret.

I pulled my notebook close to me, the one that held Mom's family stories, some but not nearly all. Stories of love in Kosice, stories of sailing from the homeland, stories of making a living in New York City and later the farm in Pennsylvania where Mom grew up in poverty, learning English and, finally, stories of Buffalo and my parents' first meeting. The stories were my personal, hard-earned collection and would help me finish the thesis that'd get me into Brown's writing program. Someday the stories would become my first novel.

Mom turned her head slowly on the pillow to face me. She was mostly bald from the chemotherapy, and her skin was dry and thin. Not long after Dr. Bilable told Mom he thought she had leukemia, he found a tumor in her breast — but it was too late for radiation to save her. The cancer had already started eating her away. I wanted to go and pull her close to me and beg her not to leave me, or us, but that'd show I was immature, weak and selfish. Mom needed me to be strong like her, not emotional like Pop. She never broke down, not when her own mother died and not now, on her deathbed.

The wind hurled swirls of painted leaves against the window and chased them across the doctors' parking lot. It was hard to believe winter had recently started, the snow fell so heavily already.

"What are you looking at?" Mom asked.

"Nothing. The street."

"Oh, Margie," whispered Mom, "don't feel so sad. Things always get better."

"I'm fine . . . I'll be okay," I assured her, though I was far from sure. How could I be, when she was abandoning me; when I didn't think, "things always get better"; when all my hard work in school and goals of being a writer were thrust aside by everyone? Was I selfish to still have dreams though Mom was dying?

"What're you thinking about?" she asked.

I tried honesty. "My book. School. Brown."

"Why?" Her voice rose slightly and I knew she didn't understand at all — not if she had to ask why. She was putting me down, so I didn't answer.

But then, maybe Mom was just anxious. "You'll have to go soon . . . The kids will be waiting, you need to make dinner and Adam's going to need more help with his home-work."

Again, I didn't say anything.

"I'm sure there's laundry too," she said.

The room was getting smaller and hotter and her prod-ding made my neck itch. I changed the subject. "Mom, will you finish the story about you living on the farm?"

"Margie, not now." She sighed. "How can you worry about that, that book now? You won't be able to get into that school anyway and it's too far away from your family."

"It's not that far! . . . And maybe you don't have that much confidence in me, but all my teachers do."

"You need to get a job and start helping out with the bills. You need to find a young man who can take care of you. None of the other girls are going to college."

"Some are . . ."

"If you decide to go to school anywhere, you can go to the University of Buffalo or community college and commute."

I couldn't believe what she was saying. Community college? The words hit me hard and I hugged my chest to stop my heart from exploding. A lump formed in my throat and I wanted to shake Mom, scream at her and blame her for ruining my life.

"I'll do what I want," I mumbled and turned away. "You won't know anyway."

"What?" she asked and I knew she hadn't heard me but

I almost wished she had. "I don't feel good. Discuss this with your father."

I realized that she had no idea that I lived in a world of a guilty conscience, where I ridiculed myself for wanting anything other than what she wanted for me.

Just then Pop's head peeked around the door, his eyes dark circles from long nights at Mom's side and long days trying to warm people's houses. Adam, the youngest, was under his arm with a good grip on Pop's belt.

Pop pointed to Mom and mouthed to me, "Can we come in?"

I nodded. With the three of us, there'd be too many in the room, but this week, on account of Mom's condition, the nurses had made an exception. Besides, the neighboring patient was out having surgery.

Pop scooted Adam towards Mom, who reached for his hands as he leaned on the bed to her. She stroked his fingers.

"Hi, Adam, sweetie," she said in a gentle whisper. Adam's birth defects, perpetual smallness and deformed thumbs, allowed him certain privileges with Mom and Pop; and warranted him a special place in my heart too.

"Hi Mom," Adam mumbled.

"Missed you, kiddo," she said quietly. "Tell me what you've been doing." Mom continued stroking his thumbs, which were actually fifth fingers. I sank into the green leather chair at the foot of the bed. Pop looked into the small mirror on the wall, plucked an eyebrow hair then turned and leaned against the wall.

"I heard you've been skipping school," Mom said.

Adam's eyes widened and he chuckled. "Awww . . . you find out everything, Mom."

"That's my job." Mom cleared her throat. A man in white stole into the room and took away the brown plastic tray, which held her hardly eaten Salisbury steak.

She rasped, "I want you to keep going to school, even when I'm not around. Especially when I'm not around. It's important, Adam, and you're no dummy."

She was being vague for Adam's sake. Her "not being around" could've meant dying or shopping at the mall. I shut my eyes to stop the burning behind them. Adam already knew though. Like Mom said, he was only eight, but he was no dummy.

"Okay, Mom, I will. Don't worry 'bout me ever. Plus, Pop's taking me around. I even learned the difference between a Buick and a Chevy!"

Lately, Pop owned his own flash-heating business and sold moonshine on the side.

"Yeah, kiddo," he said. "But Mom wants you to go to school so you don't end up like me." Pop didn't learn good job skills from his own father, my Italian grandpa, who wavered between being a plumber and unemployed.

"Oh, honey." Mom released Adam's hand and fished in the air for Pop's hand. "Don't say that, you're being silly now."

Pop moved closer to the bed and grabbed Mom's searching hand. He kissed her forehead and whispered something in her ear. She whispered back. Still gripping her hand, he looked hard at her for a minute or two. Then he turned to me and I saw rivulets of sweat streaming down his forehead. He'd just found out what was different about her, and what I'd known all day:

Mom was blind.

Pop squinted then nudged Adam toward me and told us to go home.

"Why can't I stay and talk?"

"'Cause you have stuff to do," Pop answered.

"Yes, but Pop, why can't Nat help? She never does anything . . ."

Pop's face reddened and his left eye twitched. He raised his voice, but only slightly. "Margie, don't even start! You're upsetting your mother and you know Nat is too young to handle it."

I hesitated. When I was younger I wouldn't have pushed him in order to save myself from the all too common insult or smack. I would retreat into my room, either literally or in my head – a safe place. But now, remembering the birth of his new and improved milder spirit, considering the new circumstances, I risked it.

"Mom just woke up, though. Pop, you only think about your . . ."

He shook his head and moved toward me. Adam hung on

to my sweater so tightly I imagined it unraveling bit by bit until it coiled on to the floor like a snake.

"Sullivan," Mom said weakly. She only called him by his full name, instead of Sam, when she was sad or serious.

Pop's voice bubbled through clenched teeth. "I said, 'Get going!' Now!" His red face stopped in front of mine and I could tell he wanted to grab me or push me but he stopped himself. His eyes almost popped out.

"Don't make me do something . . ." he began, then stopped again. "Don't." Maybe he prayed or thought about God peering down at him. Reading the Bible had done him a lot of good during the last year or so.

I felt guilty for stepping out of line when Pop didn't bully me so I bowed my head, took Adam's hand and walked toward the door.

But then I thought: You have no right: not after what you did to us kids and Mom. Not after you left because you thought you loved another woman more than us, not when Mom's tears came about through your flirtatious winks.

"Bye, Mom," Adam said.

"Bye," I said as I rounded the corner and peeked back at Pop, who was watching me with bulging eyes and hands on his hips. He was confusing the last few years, but I was glad he came back to us. Maybe he'd support me again like he did once before.

It had been the same time last year. I'd just gotten home from an Honor's society meeting at school. The girls weren't home yet so I could practice my cello alone in the bedroom. But soon after I had started a Saint-Saëns piece I heard Mom and Pop fighting, again. Pop's voice was loud and deep and Mom's sounded like a cat screeching.

"Why can't you be reasonable for once, Sullivan?" Mom shouted.

I opened my door and made my way down the upstairs hallway. I passed Andre's closed door and I knew that inside there he was closing the war out with his headphones. I was different, though. I wanted to know what the battle was each time, what made them hate each other or us kids.

I stopped walking when Mom's voice rose up from the kitchen. "Rhode Island? Who does she think she is?"

"She's the smartest girl in her class! She got a 1560 on her SATs! Her guidance counselor thinks she has a real chance."

"Her guidance counselor is more important than her family?" Mom yelled.

I pressed my back against the wall. My ears burned. This was their first big argument since Pop came back; and they were fighting about me. Was he really on my side?

"They don't know her," Mom said more quietly. "Now she's going to have her head in the clouds working on that ridiculous project . . . She has enough to do, and I need her here to help with the kids. She belongs with us. We're her *family*."

"Dammit, Maria, she's got to have her own life."

"Like you, huh? So she can abandon her family like you did?"

"You—!" he started. "You said you'd never bring that up again. Are you throwing it back in my face?"

Mom was silent.

"Someone's gotta go to Brown and why shouldn't it be our daughter?" Pop shouted.

I started down the hall again, avoiding the spots of the hardwood floor that squeaked so they wouldn't know I was listening.

"We can't afford it," she said.

Pop's voice steadied. "No, but she can get a scholarship. The world is different now. You can't make money anymore without a higher degree."

"Well you certainly don't! You want to send your daughter to Brown . . . Why? So you can show off to your friends who don't give a damn about you or her anyway. . ."

His voice shook the pictures on the stairway wall. "Shut up! Stop badmouthing my friends!"

"You shut up!" Mom retorted. She was really pushing it now.

"How dare you . . ." he said.

I waited for the sound of Mom's body being thrust up against the plaster wall, for the crash of a plate, a glass or a sugar bowl. Glass and grunts, thuds and ruptures.

Instead there was a moment of silence and then Mom's hopeless, almost sad voice. "She can't go! I couldn't bear it!"

I prayed that Pop wouldn't hurt her even though she was stomping on my plan to go to Brown. There was more behind her refusal than the money.

I'd reached the stairway, so I slowly got down on my knees, grasping the hard edges of the top stair for support. I eased my way on to the floor and looked down at the descending stairway. There was a space between two rungs of the railing close enough to see Mom and Pop in the dining room, but I was still out of their view.

"Yes she will go!" Pop shouted.

"No she won't!"

"Shutup, Maria!"

Mom pulled out a chair and sat down. Her voice faltered and I knew she was crying. "Fine, let her apply. Let her go . . . I just can't fight like this. It's killing me, Sam."

The house was quiet. I closed my eyes and held my breath as the silence lingered, but it stretched out so long I finally had to take some air. I slipped stealthily back up the stairs and returned to my room. Mom had said yes. I would go to Brown. My future looked bright. But as I returned the bow to my strings and began to play, tears streamed down my cheeks.

* * *

I could smell him before he even got there. Not because of potency but because of extreme familiarity — I saw Marc every day at school, and oftentimes after school, and his cologne always traveled with him. It was a fresh cool water smell that reminded me of scuba-diving and Acapulco, though I'd never experienced either.*

The evening curl of air carrying his scent swept through my window as I was slipping on a long gauze dress, empire-waist, which was patterned with subtle sunflowers. Then I heard something clatter against the window, skid down the siding and thud in the driveway. Legacy, the neighbor's dog, coughed up a bark. Though the venetian blind was cocked enough for me to lean and peek outside, my bedroom light was on so I couldn't see anyone below. There was only the driveway, an untenable plane being overcome by neglected pachysandra. Too many shadows; I heard a grated whisper.

"Psst . . . Let down your hair. I'm comin' up." I thought of the afternoon of laundry, cooking, and running after the kids and its toll on my face. I thought of my fine, mousy brown hair, needing a trim. This wasn't one of those fairy-tale moments, but Marc wasn't exactly the leading man either — he was my best friend.

"Shh . . . No, you can't. I'm getting dressed."

"Even better." Pause. "Oh, come on, Margie!"

"Pop'll be home any minute . . ."

---

* The male Danaide butterfly travels from one flower to another, collecting scents in a pocket on each hind leg until he creates the ultimate perfume to attract a female.

I heard a "mmmph" and a clang. Marc was scaling the gutter. I backed away from the window, quickly surveyed the room, and stashed some stray panties under the bed. I locked the bedroom door in case the kids came up, tired of the tube or needing a snack.

Marc tapped on the screen with two fingers. "Anybody home?"

I walked back to the window and hoisted up the screen. "Go away."

"I wanna show you somethin'."

"I'm getting ready for my writer's group meeting. Remember?"

"Great. I'll help."

I backed away from the window and a disheveled Marc heaved himself through, sliding headfirst on to the floor with a clunk. He straightened himself out and stood up to face me. Marc was a spiky blond-haired, blue-eyed German, tall and muscular, with just a slight slouch, but enough of one that made you want to push his shoulders back and straighten them. He wore his trusty navy pea coat, with a silk lining that was hanging down in the back, and black combat boots, which were liberally spotted with multicolored paint. An artist at work.

Marc silently returned my stare as he slid his coat off and let it fall to the floor. He deliberately unbuttoned his red plaid shirt and pulled both arms through, first his left, then his right. All that was left was a crisp white T-shirt and green army pants. He grinned, holding in his secret, and yanked the T-shirt over his head. His chest was broad and hairless.

My breathing got heavier. He stepped toward me and I shifted from side-to-side.

I heard Pop's voice in my head, warnings I'd heard many times before: *Marc is secretly in love with you. Stay away from him. He's got a wild streak. He's always up to no good. Whatever you do, don't let him in your bedroom.*

Marc winked at me, then spun around, revealing his stark white back.

"Marc, it's . . . it's HUGE!" I began to laugh and he laughed too, and I was still staring at his back. "I can't believe you actually . . ."

He'd gotten a tattoo. A big old, red, white and blue tattoo. A 4″ × 10″ Cat-in-the-Hat smack in the middle of his back.

"I can't believe you did that . . ."

"What's the big deal? I've always wanted one."

"Well . . . it's neat. Really. I mean, I'm a big Dr. Seuss fan."

Marc grabbed his clothes off the floor and redressed.

"How're things? How's your mom?" he asked.

"The same. Not much worse, but not better either." I lowered my voice to a whisper. "Marc, I . . . it's just so hard."

Inside I replayed the altercation with Pop at the hospital earlier that day. I wanted to tell Marc about the darkness that invaded my life, about the way it bore into me. I needed to release the feelings that had collected dust inside me from many years of not sharing and showing – to relieve some of the internal chaos. I needed someone to take the pain and cradle it, if only for a minute, so I could be a like a small child again.

But it wasn't that easy.

"Mom's blind now. She's vomiting all the time, and I'm there all the time and it's so hard but it's not her fault, you know? It just isn't. I've got to be strong and responsible for all of us because no one else can . . . Pop's a wreck too, and he's driving me absolutely . . . Oh, it must be so hard for him."

"You can do it, Margie. You're so strong. You just need a break once in a while . . . Go shoot pool with me?" Marc held his left eye in a wink and pretended he was sliding a cue along his thumb.

"You're a nutcase. Get lost." I socked him in the shoulder, but he hardly budged. He made himself comfortable on my unmade bed and I turned away to meet my face in the mirror.

"You're turning into an old lady," he said.

"Compared to the hell on wheels I used to be?" I joked. But Marc was right: in the last year I'd somehow been transported through time from young womanhood to middle age.

He laughed as I looked over my shoulder at him and lifted my brows.

"Nice dress," he said.

"Thanks."

I reached into my cosmetic bag and pulled out two lipsticks: one was purple, and the other red. I thought I should wear the red, but I wondered if fixing up was worth it. What was the purpose of exteriors anyway? Façades, overlays? And how many coats of lipstick does a woman apply until she realizes that cosmetics can't hold off cracks and wrinkles, that they're only part of her routine denial of a temporal existence? Eventually the lipsticks will be rolling around in her drawer, back-and-forth, back-and-forth, as she lies on her deathbed, pale-faced and stricken with age. But at what point does the body cross that boundary and move from lifelike to lifeless?

"You need some lipstick," Marc told me, as if he'd heard my thoughts.

I smiled, glad for his encouragement. "Okay . . . What color should I wear? *Lust* or *Power*?"

"Geez! Are you kidding? Wear 'em both."

"What a help you are."

"Wear red. You look good in red. You have nice full lips," he said.

"And so do you, I must confess." I began smoothing on the *Power*, as Marc watched from the sidelines. I heard Mom's voice in my head, cajoling as many times before: *You should hang on to that boy. You should marry Marc. He'd make a great husband. You're perfect for each other.*

"Time for your weekly poem?"

"Yeah, but I've got to go soon."

It was a ritual we started when we were both in Eighth Grade. Once a week Marc read me a poem, during our lunch break or on the side of a country road during a drive, or hanging out in my room or on the swings at the park. Then by the end of the week it was my task to uncover the mystery poet, and if I guessed wrong I had to write an original poem. This scenario would all be very romantic, but only for those who didn't know that Marc and I were simply friends. I didn't love him. Not like that. I'd known him since we were four, when his mother, Sylvia, and Mom started playing Yahtzee and chain-smoking together.

I watched Marc's reflection as he reached into his back pocket, pulled out a tiny square of notebook paper and unfolded it slowly, corner by corner.

He cleared his throat. I closed my eyes, gathered air, and let the words charge over me:

'At every instant, one must fly – like
eagles, like houseflies, like days:
must conquer the rings of Saturn*
and build new carillons there.
Shoes and pathways are no longer enough,

---

* Chunks of ice – some the size of a house, others like a grain of sand – make up the hundreds of thousands of rings around the planet Saturn. To the unaided eye, Saturn looks like a bright orange-yellow star. *See Encyclopaedia Britannica.*

the earth is no use anymore to the wanderer:
the roots have already crossed through the night,
and you will appear on another planet,
stubbornly transient,
transformed in the end into poppies.'

The poem swept through my nostrils, nuzzled behind my
eyeballs and nestled in my mind. I saw myself floating naked
and winged above the greenish light of Saturn, which was
speckled with bunches of bright red poppies. I gazed out
through gargantuan insect eyes, carried by a lifting wave of
a cloud toward the distant stars. Then I heard the bells.

"Margie?" Marc called. "I think someone's at your door."

"What?" I opened my eyes and saw Marc lying back on
my bed, propped up by pillows.

"That's probably Pop getting home . . . He usually for-
gets his key."

I grabbed my bag and went for the door.

"Should I wait here?" he asked sarcastically.

"You've got to go . . . back out the window. And don't
let him hear you!" I pulled his arm to make him stand up.

"I'll see you in the morning," I said quietly as I tiptoed to
the door. "If you don't skip class again."

"Ciao, bella."

"Coming!" I yelled as I bolted down the stairs. I saw Pop's
nose pressing against the glass pane of the door window. As
I approached his face gradually disappeared behind a patch

of fog forming from his breath and I saw only sprouts of black hair. I swung open the door.

Pop came through slowly, like a wounded soldier, sallow-faced with arms stiff at his sides and legs dragging. On the way to the coat closet he met my eyes and paused, staring as though he'd never seen me before. I suddenly became aware of the cold breeze coming through the door that I held open. I closed it a little, turned, and watched Pop hang his overcoat in the overstuffed closet.

"Margie, can I talk to you for a second?" he asked.

"Sure, what's up?" I said lightly, to cut the solemnity. After all, no hard feelings.

He trudged into the living room and sank into the arm-chair. I closed the door and followed him, then sat opposite him, on the couch.

"This isn't easy, not for any of us, especially Mom. I'd appreciate it if you'd be more agreeable."

"Of course," I said.

"Is that a problem?"

Yes it's a problem, I began in my head, but what I said was, "No, Pop."

"Margie, is there something you want to say to me? I want to know how you're feeling."

"About what?" I tilted my head and twirled my hair.

"About this, all this. Everything."

Right now? I thought. *I've known you seventeen years and you ask me about my feelings now, when my mom's dying and I'm on my way out the door? Where do I begin?* All through the years I'd wanted him to say something, to give me an excuse to open up to him, and when he didn't, that was oppressive. But now, by being direct, that seemed oppressive too.

As I groped for something to say, the bird stuck his head out of the clock's chateau and coo-cooed, then "Edelweiss" began to play. Afterward, the silence seemed to last hours. I couldn't say a word – my lips felt heavier and my throat closed up so much my ears popped. Finally, Pop spoke.

"Well, I just want to say that I've been thinking about some things lately, mostly about the future and my relationship with you kids. Mom's really kept us together, you know?" He lifted his hands and rubbed his head. His eyelids twitched, and I thought he was going to cry. "If it hadn't been for her strength . . . Well, I just might not have come back."

I wasn't shocked to know this, to hear him say it. Of course I'd already known, but Pop was right – Mom stuck it out and she got twenty-six years of marriage. Not bad. I just wondered if it was worth it, for her or for us.

He sighed. "I'm sorry for hurting your mother over the years, I really am."

My voice shook. "Why are you telling me this? Why aren't you telling *her*?"

"I've tried . . . Yes"

Yeah, but it's too late now, I thought. *It's just too late. She needed you long ago.*

". . . And I'm sorry if I've hurt you too, Margie. I know I haven't been very close to you emotionally, and I've raised my voice a few times but . . ."

A few times? Raised your voice? And what about the times you dragged me by my hair? It was all too much for me. I stared at the wall and my eyes got lost in the swirls of paisley, a bevy of amebas swimming around and around in a pool of green slime.

Pop's voice cracked. "Mom doesn't have much longer. They're going to up her morphine." His eyes shrank and filled with tears. "I know you're concerned about your life right now, your goals and your writing, but you'll need to set it aside for awhile. I'm going to need you . . ." He seemed to collapse in the chair, sucked down into the cushions like spilled coffee seeping into carpet. "You're my only hope. Please."

I rose weakly from my seat and stared at the top of Pop's head. He was bent over with his hands in his thick hair, and it was the first time I'd ever looked down at him. It felt good.

Part of me wanted to touch him, talk to him, peek out from my mask, but showing my anger over his expectations or sorrow over my selfish behavior would paint me weak. In showing it, in saying "Here it is, Pop, my discontent!" I'd make both my weakness and my unhappiness something unavoidable. I'd make the demon real. So instead, I slipped into what was comfortable and familiar – my mask of a plastic smile and hollow eye. The perfect automaton.

"Pop, it's okay. It's going to be okay," I said, and walked toward the door. Glancing back at him, our eyes met and I thought of Mom. "Try not to be sad."

Then I went quietly, but as I did my heart grew softer, and the weight of the house crushed me. I stood and contemplated it for a moment: red brick, the ivy growing over it, and the birds that nested there. I wished for the call of the mourning dove but, greeted by silence, was glad for the breeze and the grey light of the moon as I walked into the night.

* * *

I got so tired sometimes, waiting.

The moon had clouded over and we expected a blizzard – Mom and I, sitting silently in the room as if we were in a concentration camp waiting to be taken to the gas chamber. If not both, at least one of us would be sucked away into another realm – and already we suffered from the loss.

"Where's your journal?" she asked, turning her head delicately away from the window. She'd had me pull back the curtains so she could watch the lightning streak up the navy sky.

"I didn't bring it," I told her. "Why?"

"I thought you wanted to hear about when your Baba got sick."

Of course. I wanted to hear, but Mom looked so tired,

struggling to keep her eyes open. "Don't worry about it. I remember a little. You told me a long time ago."

"I know, but it's important."

Her face was pasty except for the few age spots on her cheeks that had blossomed over the last few years. Seeing them as large beautiful freckles emphasizing her high cheek-bones made me wonder why she used to cover them faithfully. She wasn't wearing lipstick either. When she was first admitted, she had the nurses put some color on her – pencil her blonde eyebrows to emphasize her deep-set eyes, blush her cheeks for a natural-looking flush. She'd given up on that too.

"Mom, are you sure? You can hardly talk."

She smiled at me with closed lips and returned her gaze to the window. Seeming to draw strength from the sky, she began:

"Baba was my age when she went mad, you know. It happened when we lived on the farm in Pennsylvania . . . She and Zedo had married before he left Kosice for America to start a life for them. She waited for him for seven years, living only on hope and a couple of letters, raising the kids by herself. Finally, when he'd saved enough money, he sent for her, and she came, but had to leave her whole family behind. She never saw them again. Then eight kids, running a farm; it must've been too much for her . . ."

I saw the picture of Baba in my head, the one taken when she left Czechoslovakia, the one that rested on our mantel.

I'd memorized it: tightened lips, vacant eyes, she wore a
scarf around her head – staring. The first two boys, nearly
identical, clung to her arms – eager, anxious, scared to
death.

"She would cry every night. Then she received a letter
informing her that her brother in Czechoslovakia had died.
She kept the letter in the pocket of her housecoat, sometimes clutching it in her hands, crying and rocking in her
chair. Zedo didn't know what to do. Their whole lives
they never went to the doctor but, finally, she got so bad he
took her, and then she wouldn't take the medicine. Milla
and I snuck pills in her Coca-Cola or her chocolate candies,
but she was so paranoid. She knew every single time and
then she'd go off in a room by herself or come after us."

"Come after you?"

"At times she'd sit really, really quiet, and other times
she'd be on a rampage. Something would set her off. She'd
chase after us through the house or the field with a broom
or a poker and we'd have to hide from her."

It came flooding back to me. Mom had told me some of
the things right after Baba had died. I'd loved listening to
her then; it meant seeing my mother as more than a care-
giver or a good cook. It meant seeing her as a real person,
someone with an imperfect past, someone with pain but
who could soar above all that. I loved hearing her now too,
yet it frightened me – there was a somber finality in her tone
and she was surprisingly lucid.

"Mom, you don't have to do this."

"The older kids and Zedo would go out some evenings so she'd ask Milla or me to sleep with her until they came home. I'd lie stiffly under the *parina* beside her, watching closely. I remember looking over and seeing her whispering and I'd think, 'Uh oh.' I knew she was hearing or thinking something that wasn't happening. I'd hold myself so still in the bed and close my eyes tightly and listen to her whisper over and over. Suddenly she'd slap me in the face with the back of her hand and say *'sihobuc, sihobuc'* which means 'shut up, shut up.'"

Mom cleared her throat, struggling. It seemed she floated above her words — like she was talking about someone else.

"What did you think? Did you know what was going on?"

"I just knew she was sick and had to help her. There was never any 'What's wrong with her?' I just felt, 'Okay, that's what I've got to live with.' My dad never thought, 'Oh I'm going to leave my wife' and I never thought, 'Oh poor me.' Once you were family, you were family. Of course I was embarrassed for her, so we didn't bring anyone up to the house anymore. Mostly I was sad. It was like I didn't have a mom anymore, and that's why I was so close to my dad."

I nodded, and tried to imagine Mom as a little girl growing into a woman, but when I did, she looked exactly like me. I moved my chair closer to the bed as her voice grew softer.

"She didn't sleep at night and would roam around. Eventually it got to the point she was so dangerous we had to sleep in the attic. Zedo secretly built a door to close us off — he had to do it without her knowing. It was a big wooden door with strong hinges that he placed over the stairs. We had to push the door up to get in, and once inside, bolting it shut, we were secure . . . at least for a little while."

As I listened I tried to remember the details, creating a chain of moments in my head that I could recall later.

"We slept in the attic awhile before she figured out we were there. When she found out, she'd bang on our door with a broom and yell at us to open up. But we'd stay quiet and wouldn't open it. She tried several times to chop it with an axe. One night I could see the door beginning to crack and I crouched in the corner, huddling with Milla.

"I felt terrible because she was our mother and we were locking her out, pushing her away, but we had to keep ourselves safe and we had no idea what she would do. One day she took an axe and chopped the door down. But by that time we'd already moved to the barn and were sleeping in the granary bins filled with straw. Even Zedo slept out there."

Before, I'd seen my mother's strength as she cooked and cleaned and catered to her eight children and her husband.

I'd seen her strength as she took care of her parents as they aged into their nineties; as she endured both of their deaths and two brothers who died from alcoholism; as she supported my father while he was out of work. But somehow this was even more.

"We put her in a hospital when we moved to Niagara Falls. I was fourteen. I remember visiting her after school and being really afraid of some of those people. But at the hospital they got her regulated on medicine. After three months, she was getting better so they let her come home for visits on the weekend. Finally they let her out but I had to watch that she took her medicine every day.

"After a while we started getting lax about giving it to her – she seemed back to normal. Eventually she wasn't taking any medicine and she started to talk to herself again. And she had super-human strength. Nothing could stop her. We called the institution again and they came down with a straitjacket. I was upstairs at the time because I didn't want to watch. I was crying so hard because I felt guilty for letting them take her, but I knew it was for the best. She was kicking and screaming, fighting the men who were trying to get the jacket on her. She didn't want to go and called out for me, 'Maria, Maria. *Ne treba!*'"

"What does that mean?"

"Not necessary."

I suddenly forgot myself the writer, and became myself the daughter, lost in the image of Mom listening as her mother was taken away. I put my hand to my chest to feel my heart like a stone, and held it there to ease the anxiety. I felt like letting go, having a hearty cry, but I didn't – for Mom's sake.

"What kept you from going crazy yourself?" I asked.

She sighed. "Acceptance. My mother was sick and she needed to get better. When I think about what I went through and how I did it so easily, I can't believe how strong I was at such a young age. But mostly, I never felt sorry for myself. I thought, 'This is what I have to do.' I did the best I could for them, always. I took care of them because they were my parents and they needed help."

How do you do that? I wondered. *How do I do that? Live matter-of-factly, not dwell on it? Is happiness gained through acceptance? Maybe it is.*

"I asked your Baba just before she died, 'Mumma, do you remember when you were sick and you thought we'd said something bad to you and you hit us?' And she said, shaking her head, 'No, Maria, no, no.' And I didn't want to tell her what happened because she'd have been awfully hurt to think that she'd hurt us . . ." Her voice trailed off, leaving the room silent except for the sound of squeaking wheels that passed along the hallway.

You're like that, Mom, I thought. She never wanted to hurt us, or watch us get hurt, so she wrapped us in a protective shell until we couldn't breathe. *Maybe that's love.* As a child I couldn't see that sometimes Mom or Pop hurt me because they were trying to show love, and as parents they couldn't see that being extra protective didn't guarantee their daughter would come out unscathed.

I rose from my chair and reached for Mom, cradling her bald head in my hands. *"Dime ruchu,"* I said and leaned to kiss her cheek. Her eyes were closed, and she was breathing steadily.

"Mom, I love you," I said quietly. "You know that, don't you? I've been so distant, so selfish. I'm sorry. It doesn't mean that I don't love you or appreciate everything you and Pop have done for me. I just need to be free. Please let me go . . . Oh, I know you never will. Not even if you . . ." I stopped, looking at her parted lips. I placed my cheek on them.

She was already gone.

It was strange: I always wanted Mom close so I could call when I needed her or grab her arm if I was falling. At the same time, it was easier to keep her at a careful distance, either one step ahead or one step behind, but usually one step behind. If I maintained my own little world where she couldn't enter I could be my own person, and have an excuse for not measuring up to being the woman she was, the woman I desired to be. If I maintained my own little world I didn't have to trust anyone but myself, and didn't suffer someone breaking that trust. I didn't get hurt and prevented myself from hurting others. Now that she had shared so much with me — and let me into her own little world – I realized we had lost something by holding out and holding in all those years. Now that I'd had a glimpse, I knew there was much more that I would never see, behind another closed door, hidden stories somewhere deep in her heart, which remained untold.

See ULU   *M. Guerriri, Rhode Island*

✳

WINTER is the season of discomfort.

J. Rimbaud, Scandinavia

✳

X-MAS, short for Christmas, dates back over 4000 years, when its early traditions began, before Christ was born. In order to convert pagans to Christianity, the Church decided that the Roman celebration of *Saturnalia* would be made into a celebration of the birthday of Christ. The Church was successful in taking the lights, gifts, merriment and masquerades from pagan festivals and incorporating them into a Christian observance. In AD 350 Julius I of Rome chose December 25 as the observance of Christmas. (The exact date of Christ's birth has never been determined. The account states that on His birth the shepherds were outside tending their flocks during the night, which they would not do during wintertime.) Formerly,

Mesopotamians celebrated their God Marduk over a festival that lasted for twelve days, and originated the traditions of bright fires, Yule logs, gift giving, parades and carolers.

Esperanto: *Gajan Kristnaskon!*

Scandinavians and Celts climbed to the mountaintops and awaited the return of the Sun. They would commemorate Yuletide with great bonfires.

Slovak: *Prejeme Vam Vesele Vanoce a statsny Novy Rok.*

In ancient times the Greeks held winter celebrations in honor of the god of wine and fertility, Dionysus; while Babylonians celebrated *Sacaea* by feasting, drinking and lovemaking.

Afrikaans: *Een Plesierige Kerfess!*

Halls decked with laurel accompanied by Lucky Fruits, called *Strenae*, were exchanged with fellow Romans, who masqueraded and lit up trees in a festival they called *Saturnalia*, which lasted from mid-December to January 1.

Ed.

❄

YODELING, not to be confused with YOKELING, reread LOST, and here's how the story begins: with a picturesque view of the Bavarian Alps, with a man in lederhosen singing . . . '*Mir san ja dö lustigen Holzhackers-*

baum, holaröh — yodel; Mir fürchten koan Teifi, koa Wetter und Sturm — yodel.' This singing man was a Baker, friend of the Butcher and the Candlestick Maker, who, unlike the Shoemaker, would not often travel from his little village of Gschaid, where the valley appears to be hedged in by rock walls, to the market-town of Millsdorf — a three-hour trek.

Not many did — in fact, months would pass, even a year, without anyone crossing the *col,** which linked two mountain ranges and, thickly studded with pines, was in itself a great mountain range. Nevertheless, one winter's morning (glaciers should be traversed before 10 a.m., he thought), the Baker rubbed his feet with brandy and tallow, to prevent abrasion whilst travelling, and set out with his rolls for the neighbouring village. No one knows exactly why he travelled that day, for excursions in the higher Alps are dangerous before July, and over all the movements of

---

* The letter C is named Coll in the Irish Ogham alphabet called the *Beth-luis-nion*, a calendrical "tree" alphabet in which each letter stands for a tree and has mystical proportions. Its tree is the hazel, the Tree of Wisdom. The other six trees in the Irish tree-alphabet correspond to the other six important letters in the alphabet. Robert Graves, in his book *The White Goddess*, suggests that the *Beth-luis-nion* came from Greece, and the names of the letters form a Greek charm in honor of the Arcadian White Goddess Alphito. These Greek letters were keys to unlocking all types of mystery:

'Α 'Ε 'Η 'Ι 'Ο 'Υ 'Ω

the pedestrian the weather holds despotic sway; perhaps he was itching to get out of town or desperate to make a good sovereign. Upon entering the *col,* the Baker noticed the ranges' two pinnacles were snow-white and the walls were coated with a thick layer of hoar-frost. He recalled that in his rucksack he carried: tincture of arnica (a good remedy for bruises), saturnine ointment (for inflammation), and glycerine (for the lips); and, as always, he wore two watches – one facing up, one facing down.

He walked briskly, up and up. The ascent was so steep that the road led east and west in a serpentine manner. Still, the Baker yodelled all the while, with a cheerful disposition, the only one who, leaving solitary footprints, appeared to be crossing the *col* that day. After two hours he reached the deep wooded portion of the *col,* with its large pines all flecked with fast-falling snow. The flakes fell thicker and thicker, covering his path, so that soon the Baker could only see the trees directly in front of him. Further, the air was still – not a limb rustled, not a hair on his head stirred, not a bird chirped in the forest. After another hour or more, he reached the summit, the mournful mountaintop, so he thought, where the glittering winter sky is forever unchanging. Soon it was dark all around, with only whiteness everywhere – an obscuring mist. The Baker looked around and twisted his back each way in each direction, but saw no escape from this avalanche of snow.

No one knows what happened then to this Baker from

Gschaid, but his yodelling, a sound that had carried all the way to his village, suddenly stopped after the storm came. Perhaps he never found his way out of the obscurity of the snow, paling into fog, which shrouded everything and then devoured him. Perhaps the cold was so bone-chilling that his lungs haemorrhaged, his jaw locked and his teeth popped out like watermelon seeds. Whatever the case may be, at the crest of the *col*, at the highest point of the road, his body was found – toppled over in the dry grass with the basket and rolls, closed eyes, grey coat, hands crossed, the pines scattered about him.

Sanna, Bavaria

Further reading: Stifter, Adalbert, *Rock Crystal*, Vienna, 1845; van der Loeff, Rutgers A., *Avalanche!*, Amsterdam 1954.

❄

ZENITH: an important aspect of the mystery of sevens, which is found among the primal people of Native North America, as well as in the Bible, where seven is used to signify the idea of completeness or unity; and in alchemy, where the seven metals equal seven bodies. The Sioux have seven sacred rites, the Ojibwa Midewiwin follow seven prophecies, cycles of seven years and seven Grandfathers. The seven Grandfathers are symbolized in the teaching staff hung in the ceremonial circle. The staff is made up of three sticks bound at their centers. The sticks have six points representing four directions plus two for sky and earth. The seventh stick is the crossing-point, the power within, the Here, the Zenith. Nature represents itself in pairs: dark and light, cold and hot, male and female. The two are not contradictory but are aspects of one; different but in balance, like the Arctic dweller with nature — cold, ice, snow. Zenith says: *all powers are available to me and moving through me, through visions and dreams.*

J. W. Newbury, Alaska

Notes

Alchemy. A calling. It expresses the conviction that the *quinta essentia* can be discovered in matter from everything that has life, then refined into its highest purity. Alchemical studies include such subjects as metals, plants, flowers, numbers, water, and snow, focusing on opposites: mind and body, love and hate, good and evil, life and death, hot and cold. The opus involves seven steps, with methods tied to illumination and imagination, death and rebirth. It begins with the transformation of the human personality, when the imagination guides the alchemist to truth – allowing one to *see* in new ways. The ultimate goal is to reunite matter and spirit in a transformed state, creating something called the Spirit (or Elixir) of Life. Some believe that those who imbibe it will prolong their lives and increase in knowledge and wisdom. Other symbols used for the reconciliation of opposites are the Philosopher's Stone or the Holy Grail.

The philosophy of alchemy has two currents: one artisanal in nature and another involving the sciences, although the strands often overlap. The alchemist and artist play the same role, according to Gaston Bachelard; "calling forth the *Materia Prima* imprisoned in opaque existence." Art is the science of awakening all matter into life through "*une rêverie parlée*," when the artist brings the inanimate world into consciousness. In *Origines de l'alchimie*, Berthelot insists that art — primarily poetry and painting — falls within the realm of "*l'haute magic*." Due to the esoteric nature of alchemy, the ways of alchemists are shrouded in secrecy. They tend to be solo practitioners who maintain their own laboratories, and rarely take pupils, unless they are secret ones — and in that case, we would never know *who* or *why*.

Ammons, Archie Randolph (1926–2001), an executive at his father's glass company in Whiteville, North Carolina. This excerpt seems to be a medley of verses found in his notebooks on Snow.

Andreyevich, Yury a.k.a. Dr. Zhivago, writes: "I did not know that my father went abroad, on one occasion, until mother told me on her deathbed. While on a rigger in the Barenes, watching the waves, father tossed a still-lit cigarette at his feet and his trousers caught fire. The flames travelled high up his leg despite attempts to beat them out, so he jumped into icy water in Archangel, Russia, down between two cargo ships in pitch darkness; and after he braved the mighty waters, the Captain of the rigger declared him an able-bodied seaman."

Authors
Multiple Choice:
A. Living **B**. Deceased **C**. Real **D**. Imagined **E**. Historical **F**. Fictional **G**. All of the above

Bailey, George, savings-n-loan, Pottersville, N.Y., 1919.

Baudelaire, Charles-Pierre.
An incomplete timeline, a list of seven:
1821 / Born in Paris, 13 rue Hautefeuille.
1838 / Expelled from school for refusing to betray a friend.
1845 / Attempted suicide.
1851 / Published on wine and hashish compared as means of augmenting personality.
1855 / Friend and poet Gérard de Nerval hanged himself from a lamppost in the rue de la Vieille-Lanterne.
1862 / Suffered a seizure.
1867 / Buried in Montparnasse.

Beyle, Marie-Henri (1783–1842), writer born in Grenoble on January 23, 1783, and who appeared on a French stamp in 1942. In 1818, he met the Countess Metilda Viscontini and fell in love with her. He confessed his love to the Countess but she would not hear him. He flooded her with letters. Finally they came to an agreement that he could visit every fortnight for one hour in the presence of others. This arrangement lasted two years, during which his love grew so unbearable that he had to flee to Milan. (It didn't help that the Austrian police were after him.)

A familiar melancholy stole upon him and he often found himself cut off from the rest of the world, on a mountain-top, surrounded by great squalls of snow driven horizontally through the air. He asked himself: *What is it that undoes a writer?* Then, in 1822, he published the semi-didactic, semi-autobiographical treatise *De l'amour*, defining crystallization in terms of that other natural force called love.

Blake, William (1757–1827), poetic genius fascinated with the moon: "There is no sun nor moon nor star, but rugged wintry rocks jostling together in the void, suspended by inward fires."

Castorp, Hans, an unassuming young man who loses his way on the Magic Mountain.

Compiler. Deceased. December 10, 2000. I knew him for seven years, the last seven of his life.

Cumming, Sandy, a kilted Highlander.

Dahmer, Jeffrey L. (1960–94), charged with twelve counts of first-degree intentional homicide after dismembered body parts were found in his freezer at his home in West Allis, Wisconsin, in 1989.

NOTES

Editor. Anon.

Eliot, Thomas Stearns (1888–1965), born in St. Louis, Missouri, educated at Harvard, moved to England and later worked as a bank clerk. Had odd jobs later in life.

Encyclop(a)ed'īa. A book of solutions giving information on all branches of knowledge or of one subject, usu. arranged alphabetically; general course of instruction; all-around education.

Ferguson, Francis. A beekeeper in Jersey.

Ferguson, Libby. A ginger-haired artist who currently lives in Manhattan.

Flaubert, Gustave (1821–1880), was known to keep his lover's mittens in his desk drawer, so he could smell them at regular intervals. This entry is a rough draft of a letter, later written with more eloquence, to Maxime Du Camp, March 15, 1846.

Furey, Michael. Died: 1887. He was a gentle boy, such a tender voice.

A gentleman who lived on 128th Street: In March 1888 a terrible blizzard dumped on the city of New York, so you couldn't even see New Jersey or Brooklyn from Manhattan. What a storm! The wind howled, banged and moaned as it rocked houses and pressed against doors. Freighted with snow, the gale (in Swedish, *frisk vind*) descended, corkscrewed, zigzagged and played havoc until the city's surface was like a battlefield. The streets were littered with horse cars intrenched in the snow, fallen street signs and broken telegraph wires. Pedestrians were strewn everywhere, having been swept off their feet, hats flying. The streets of New York were filled with a chorus of shouts, curses and screams as those who attempted to brave the wind had the breath driven down their throat. A cab driver who drove the gentleman who lived on 128th Street, and himself lived on 84th Street, commented, "I'm an old N.Y. tough. I've lived here, man and boy, all my life, but I'll be damned if ever I seen the likes o' this ride, an' I doan' wanter."

Gray, Lucy. Met William Wordsworth, poet, and his sister Dorothy, in Germany, during the exceptionally cold winter of 1798–9. She dwelt among the untrodden ways until she disappeared in the year 1800.

Griselda of Hohenkrähen. The mistress of a dwarf named Poppolinus or Poppele, as he was termed. On the outskirts of Achern, on the main line from Freiburg to Baden-Baden and near Ottersweier, you will find the ruins of Castle Windeck. One of the many legends originating in this area, as we were told in a pub in the eastern Alps, concerns the Lady of Lauf.

Guerriri, Margie. Poet Laureate of Chad.

Guerriri, Stella is a synesthete who tastes honey when she sees the color green. This sensory blending allows her to identify certain sounds or tastes with shapes or colors, similar to Rimsky-Korsakov – for whom C major was white and E major was sapphire blue – Nabokov, Baudelaire and Dylan Thomas. Synesthesia – from the Greek *syn* (together) and *aisthanesthai* (to perceive) – is a scientific term that indicates a disordering of the senses.

Hooke, Robert (1635–1703). After the good doctor died in London in 1703, his papers and manuscripts were entrusted to Richard Waller, who published them in *The Posthumous Works of Robert Hooke*. When Waller died, Hooke's belongings were passed to William Derham, who finally published *Philosophical Experiments and Observations*, containing his studies of ice, in 1726.

Hörnell, Anna Svartabjørn lives in coastal Helgeland, Norway, with its Syv Søstre (Seven Sisters) mountain range – an altitude of 1072 m. Her second name, Svartabjørn, means 'black bear' and comes from her great-great-grandmother – a dark and beautiful woman who was known to cook meals for the navvies of the Ofoten line at the end of the nineteenth century. She would often walk the tracks with the workers between Ofotenfjord and the Swedish border, during which time she met and fell in love with a young man. After she had given birth to a son, she discovered that the man had another woman; and she too was discovered, and therefore beaten to death by the navvies with a laundry paddle.

Ibsen, Henrik (1828–1906), wrote his last drama, *When We Dead Awaken*, in 1899. In it he describes the life of estranged artist Professor Rubek, who forsakes his only love, his youth and his happiness.

Kandinsky, Wassily (1866–1944), a mystic who wrote *On the Spiritual in Art* in 1912, and believed in the *Gesamtkunstwerk*, or the total work of art. According to Kandinksy, music and color appeal to the artist's "internal element" and express spiritual values. He explains his theory in this way:

Colour has symbolic meaning which resonates through the other senses. White is a symbol of a world in which there is a great, eternally cold silence, the pause before the Creation of all things that is one with numerous possibilities. In contrast, black is the dead silence which is stretched out into eternity, without hope – the place where the circle ends.

Krafft-Ebing, Richard von (1840–1902). The best-trained neuropsychiatrist on the continent in 1870, who wrote *Psychopathia Sexualis,* a volume on sexual deviation. My first question after encountering this entry was: What does this have to do with snow? I entered the mind of the compiler, I scrounged for the connections . . . winter garments serving as fetishes. Hmmm. Did he have a fetish? No. Did he want to reveal his disgust for such behavior? Perhaps. Better yet, he discovered that snow worlds are breeding grounds for unusual cases. So I think.

The Lady-in-Waiting to the Empress Ulu lived at the end of the tenth century, and was a contemporary of Lady Murasaki Shikibu, the greatest figure in Japanese literature and author of *The Tale of Genji*. It is rumoured that the lady-in-waiting was a lover to the Emperor Kikō, and wrote these poems in the few weeks after his death and before her own. Nothing else is known of her except what can be gathered from her work. For example, her final poem, VII, suggests that she yearned for her lover so much she drifted into death: It refers to "The River of Heaven," a mythical name for the Milky Way galaxy, where the magpies link their wings and form a bridge by which true lovers can cross. On the seventh night of the seventh month, the Herd Boy, Altair, crosses the galaxy to meet the Weaving Girl, Vega, from whom he is separated for the rest of the year.

Lola–Lola. A dancer at the Blue Angel Club during the 1940s. She was said to look like the actress Marlene Dietrich.

London, Jack (1876–1916). Born in San Francisco, California, in 1876, as John Griffith Chaney, believed to be the bastard of William Chaney, astrologer and journalist, who abandoned Jack's mother Flora, a spiritualist. Flora married John London, a Civil War veteran, when Jack was eight months old. Jack was a laborer, an oyster pirate, a sailor, a railroad hobo, a gold prospector. It was during his travels across America that he learned about socialism. In 1900, Jack married his math tutor, Bess Maddern. They had two daughters: Joan and Betsy. In 1903, Jack separated from Bess and married his secretary and soulmate, Charmian Kittredge, with whom he played, traveled, wrote and lived until his death by uremic poisoning in 1916. His writings have been translated in several dozen languages and continue to be read throughout the world.

Massak, meaning "soft snow" in Labradoran Inuit, married to Sikko ("ice") with two children, Pukak and Aput ("snow like salt" and "snow in general"), but her heart still longs for her Nanuq ("polar bear"), who died the day after he kissed her for the first time.

Meeko, Bella, explains: "An ulu is a crescent-shaped knife Inuit women use for skinning animals, preparing skins, eating, sewing and butchering. As a kamik-maker, I would be lost without my ulu: I use it to remove blubber from seal skin, shave hair from caribou skin, even to eat muktak. It takes a very long time to sharpen if someone lets it get too dull. When I die, my ulu will be buried with me."

Miano, Sarah Emily. After suffering from a concussion for two months, during Sixth Grade, she resumed her studies at Payne Street School. Drew Davidson, this time with a little bit of hair (he was now playing lead as Henry Higgins), escorted her to the Winter Holiday Dance and kissed her like no man had kissed her since Mark (a.k.a. Spud) Webb, after offering him her celery stick.

Miller, Snowdrop. The story continues: Still no sign of my father, and mother waited all night. The contractions began soon after 6 a.m., eventually surging through her in quick bursts like BB shots. I must have been anxious to come out. Suddenly, mother heard him call for her, and she yelled back, "Help! I'm in here!" Soon the men were digging her out with shovels – she could hear them scrambling against the door. Mother clutched herself in pain, thinking, *Please Lord, please please*. But they got her out soon enough; and she rode on the back of a plow that pushed through the deep snow all the way to Sioux City Hospital, where she gave birth to me – a blonde-haired, blue-eyed snow child – at approximately 10:03 a.m.

Monet, Claude (1840–1927). Painter who moved with his family from Paris to Vétheuil in 1878. After an unsuccessful abortion, his wife, Camille, died on September 5, 1879, aged thirty-two years. Monet recounts that on that September day, before the long winter, when the first light had entered the room, he sat at the bedside of his dead wife. His gaze was fixed on her tragic temples, and he observed the shades and nuances of color that Death brought to her face – blues, grays and yellows in her hair. "Against my will," he said, "my reflexes took possession of me in an unconscious process." He then painted his Great Work, a personal record of the darkest hour, *Camille Monet on her Deathbed*.

Moth and Butterfly. A pair of lovers whose true identities have remained undiscovered and have stirred up much speculation by historians because their writing styles are so similar that the letters seem to be a work of fiction by one author.

Nabokov, Vladimir (1899–1977), felt that nature and art were forms of magic, games of intricate enchantment and deception. He further writes: "I have hunted butterflies in various climes and disguises: as a pretty boy in knickerbockers and sailor cap; as a lanky cosmopolitan expatriate in flannel bags and beret; as a fat hatless old man in shorts . . . It is astounding how little the ordinary person notices butterflies. 'None,' calmly replied that sturdy Swiss hiker with Camus in his rucksack when purposely asked by me for the benefit of my incredulous companion if he had seen any butterflies while descending the trail where, a moment before, you and I had been delighting in swarms of them."

Nakaya, Ukichiro. A Japanese meteorologist who took 2500 photomicrographs of snow crystals and classified them by mass, speed of fall and electrical nature into seventy-seven categories. He and his team successfully produced every known type of snow crystal in a cold chamber, in a laboratory, in the 1940s. In the 1880s, William Bentley, a Vermont farmer, photographed 7000 ice crystals with a box camera.

Newbury, J. W. Professor of Native Studies, University of Anchorage, Alaska.

Nussbaumer, Eva.
By post, a letter:
Dear Eva,
When I left you I drove to the lake, now frozen over, taking Hemingway's Garden of Eden *with me. The sun was strangely warm for a day that had begun in such chill, but it wasn't uncomfortable sitting there with the liquid gold pooling around me. As I read I saw that yes, Catherine is you, or maybe she is the woman inside Hemingway, a part of him he could never accept. She always lives for the moment of each day, believing that the next will never*

touch her as long as she can do whatever she wants right now. But she always scrutinizes herself, feeling the need to shed her skin and grow some new. Her lover recognizes her perfection but knows that she will always change because her own introspection drives her to it, and introspection will always find flaws no matter how perfect the object of inspection. Our greatest challenge it seems, dear Eva, especially if we have been told while young that we were flawed, is to not only forgive our own imperfections but to smile at them, squint, fuzz the hard edges and see them as an endearing part of our ourselves.

I find you beautiful.

J.D.

Oates, Capt, not to be confused with *Quaker Oats*, officially formed in 1901 when several oat-milling pioneers united to give America a superior oats product. One of these pioneers was Ferdinand Schumacher, known as the Oatmeal King, who founded German Mills American Oatmeal Co. in 1856.

Oddbody, Clarence. Guardian angel, Second Class, a streaking star.

Paulina, an American in France was named from Pierre-Jean Jouve's classic 1880 novel: *Oh no, dear butterfly, watch out for the flame. Look! Another one is about to die like last night . . . another one right now! It comes back to the fire in spite* *of itself, because it doesn't understand fire, its betrayal; one wing is already burned, but it comes back, again and again. That's fire, my poor butterfly. That's fire.*

Pavlovski, Molly Jo. An American woman passing through Liverpool Street Station, who is eager to find her seat on the train, loses a piece of paper hanging from her pocketbook, which catches in the wind and gets blown along the dusty platform. Later, a man who sees it fluttering near his bench picks it up and places it surreptitiously in his pocket. After reading it with his coffee on the train, he ascribes these characteristics to the unknown woman: Sagittarius, enjoys getting French manicures, line-dancing, walking her dog Timmy, toy poodle, and attending social galas for her +50 gardening club, *Tampa Tarts for Tulips, Inc.* © 1999.

Peck, Rev. Julian, Moravian missionary, apostle to the Eskimos, supported by the British Government for operating mission stations in the Inuit homeland to provide Eskimos with European goods in exchange for their souls. (Aid given by missionaries to the ill, elderly, orphaned and hungry led to increasing numbers of Inuit abandoning their spiritual beliefs for Christianity in the nineteenth century.)

Petrarch, Francesco, born in 1304, lost his beloved Laura in death.

Plath, Sylvia. Born in 1932 in Boston, Massachusetts. While on a Fulbright to Newnham College, Cambridge, she met Ted Hughes, poet, whom she married in 1956. Her first book, *The Colossus*, was published in 1960. After a period in the United States, she settled in England where her two children were born. She said, "Maybe forgetfulness, like a kind snow, should numb and cover them."

Protocol of the Deceased, recording the death of a certain man named Vivaldi, who composed a piece in honor of winter: Concerto 4, "Inverno," from *The Four Seasons*, in F Minor from a longer set of twelve, Opus 8, called "The Trial Between Harmony and Invention." When questioned why a great composer was buried in a place for executed criminals, the President of the Protocol, Victor Hoffmann, exclaimed: "We bury the dead as soon as possible, quite often on the very day of death. We only make exceptions for prominent persons, never paupers. What a stink! Take them far outside the city!"

Ramblin' Lou Family Singers, The, include: Lou Lou (Sr.) on banjo and vocals; Joni Mitchell Lou on ukulele; Lou Lou (Jr.) on percussion; Linda Lou on washboard and harmonica; Eliza Lou on spoons. We met them in Scarborough, Ontario; saw them playing in a restaurant while we dined on falafel. While I didn't sing along, my friend, the compiler, joined the band on zither. (In case you have never encountered a zither — one usually doesn't — it is a plucked or struck stringed instrument with a shallow soundbox placed on one's knees or on a table. The player's left hand stops the melody strings on the fretted keyboard while the right hand plucks with the fingers and a thumb plectrum. It sounds simple, but I assure you: it isn't.)

Rimbaud, Jean (1854–1891), was born in 1854 at Charleville, France. Later he travelled as an interpreter for the circus in Scandinavia.

Rimsky-Korsakov, Nikolai composed *The Snow Maiden*, the story of an Icewoman who is the result of the mismatched union between Frost and Spring.

Sanna. Our Alpine guide in Bohemia. She introduced us to the surroundings before the climb: "We received 80 cm of fresh snow in the mountains today. The Alpine rock is in good shape as long as one stays on southerly exposures. The forecast for the next five days is a series of fronts and talk of the *Föhn,* but we are hoping to avoid this. More snow is predicted for the west and south, so we may get lucky. When we reach the top, I will tell you the myth about the Baker from Gschaid, as we will be passing his memorial, the red post, at the highest point on the *col* . . . I wonder if a snowflake in an avalanche ever feels responsible."

Sansone, Stella. "Single flame, I am alone."

Scarecrow. a Roman deity on the Esquiline Hill – the
highest and largest of seven in Rome, along with the Capi-
toline, Palatine, Velia, Quirinal, Celian and Oppian. The
Esquiline Hill is famous for the miraculous snowfall that
occurred on its summit in the summer of 352 during the
pontificate of Liberius. According to legend, Roman patri-
cian John and his wife prayed on the evening of August 5 for
a sign indicating how they should dispose of their property
in honor of Our Lady. Later that night, John's wife saw a
vision of a woman in white standing on the Esquiline. After
she composed herself, the snow fell and therefore, considering it a most potent sign, the couple built a basilica on the
very spot, giving it the official name *Dedicatio Sanctæ Mariæ
ad Nives* or Our Lady of the Snow.

Shay and Dora. A modern-day mythological pair. Their
story is based on the remnants of their journals found
posthumously.

Snow, Robert Esq. From Sept. 1834 to Sept. 1839 he
made a series of observations of the aurora borealis, veils
of light caused by solar wind reacting with the earth's
magnetic field. He concluded from his studies that the
aurora borealis, or northern lights, are the result of solar
winds flowing past and elongating the earth's magnetic
field. Charged particles are drawn toward the earth to inter-
act with electrons in the upper atmosphere, which release

N O T E S

energy and create the visible aurora. They may be expected during any time of the year, and assume all colors and forms, whether haloes, pillars, or wisps; whether undulating, radiating, glittering, or streaming.

The display is wholly inaudible, Snow argues. The arousal at the sight of these phenomena tricks the viewer and fools their other senses; so that these "fibs of vision" lead the viewer to feel, hear and smell strange things at the instant of their occurrence. However, Snow concedes, they are simply illusions caused by the sight of astonishing beauty. The esoteric nature of these sights can perhaps explain why the Inuit call the lights "to play with ball," and considered them gifts from the dead to light the long nights. Other natural phenomena in this category are *parhelia* – images that form on either side of the sun near the horizon in extremely cold temperatures. Positioned on the halo, they are caused by the refraction of light through ice crystals with their axes aligned vertically. These images are commonly referred to as sun dogs or mock suns.

Staël, Germaine, Madame de, (1766–1817), the daughter of Jacques Necker, minister of finances to Louis XVI. Her definition of happiness was "the union of all contrary things." Although she had many intense friendships and love relationships, her most important was with Benjamin Constant, a liberal politician whom she met in Switzerland in 1794. Both Constant and Staël suffered from an *inquiétude* or melancholy stemming from the inadequacy of all objects of desire. They believed in the possibility of complete emotional intimacy by means of "transparency," as Rousseau called it, or a natural form of communication between true lovers. This transparency can be compared to the fur on a polar bear, which appears white to the human eye.

Waterhouse, John William (1847–1917), description of his painting, *Saint Eulalia*, 1885, oil on canvas, 188.6 × 117.5 cm. Exhibited Tate Gallery, London. Saint Eulalia of Mérida (d. 304?) was a virgin martyr, girl of twelve, arrested and tortured by the magistrate because she would not denounce the Christian faith in favor of pagan idol worship. Prudentius wrote a hymn in her honour in 405, revealing the signs of her innocence: the departure of "a sudden snowy-white dove," and the miraculous snowfall which concealed her body from onlookers. Saint's Day: December 10.

Whipple, Fred Lawrence (1906–?). Astronomer raised on an Iowa farm who introduced his dirty-snowball theory in 1950. Edmond Halley concluded from the sightings of comets, occurring in intervals of seventy-seven years, that all of them were the same comet travelling an elliptical orbit. The Bayeux Tapestry, which commemorated the Norman victory with seventy scenes, depicts Halley's

Comet as a scintillating star having a multiple tail, being pointed at by onlookers below.

Williams, Luke, lives in South Tyrol, studying the 1000 Yeti beasts along with his team of assistants in the Himalayas. Williams was the second climber to scale Mount Everest without the aid of bottled oxygen, singing, "Heigh Ho, Heigh Ho . . . "

YHWH, *JHVH,* the Tetragrammaton, four-letter Hebrew designation written as Yahweh or, in English, Jehovah; the sacred name of the God of Israel which was revealed to Moses, the God of the Judeo-Christian tradition. The name is a verb, the causative form, the imperfect state meaning "He Who Causes To Become." The holy name of God was considered too sacred to pronounce – with vowels, signs or sounds, thus *YHWH* was rendered and later *Adonai* or Lord in the Scriptures; still, modern translators substitute the original Tetragrammaton for LORD 6828 times in the Old Testament alone.

Epilogue

The rucksack merits my complete trust. A brown leather bag slung by straps from both of my shoulders, it rests on my back, and has accompanied me everywhere: through the Alps, the Apennines and the Arctic Circle.

Contents:

An iron key

A cream-colored, polka-dotted handkerchief

An old photograph of a Swiss boy

A vial of perfume containing a scent that reminded him of his dead wife

A journal, tied-up with string

An iron key

An instrument that gives opportunity for, or precludes access to something, for example: the lock on a secret laboratory. Other definitions for key include:

1. A solution, explanation, or book of solutions.

2. (Musical) A system of notes based on a particular style, tone, thought or expression
3. One essential to the carrying on of others; the central principle on which all depends

The iron key is heavy in my rucksack. I take it out and cradle it in my palm. My fingers travel over all its contours, along the shaft then its intricate grooves. The iron key is heavy in my hand.

A cream-colored, polka-dotted handkerchief

A square of silk, carried in the rucksack for wiping my nose, dabbing my brow or wearing about my neck — also called a *neckerchief* — but not always in my possession.

Let me explain.

The second-to-the-last time I saw him we met in Helsinki and dined on any kind of food that could be dried, smoked, salted or preserved: reindeer tongue, jellied eels, herring salad, smoked eels, boiled ox tongue, pig's feet, salmon in aspic.

After we finished this *Smörrebröd*, he assured me that my metabolism would surely increase by 30 percent.

He offered me a cigarette. Then he took one for himself, struck a match, lit my cigarette and his own.

Let me tell you a story, he said.

Okay, I said, sat back and readied myself for a good one.

It is about a courtesan from Cadiz named Caroline . . .

This was out of character.

. . . a woman who lit men's faces with desire to hear her voice, which seemed more avian than human.

I'm interested.

I know this because I knew her once.

Yes, I am *very* interested. I pushed the half-eaten veal brawn across the plate with my fork.

I first saw Caroline at a performance of *Carmen* at the Royal Albert Hall, where she was singing the title role. Despite my timidity, I was moved so deeply by her dulcet voice that when she finished I joined the audience in clapping and shouting, "Bravo!" I was compelled to go backstage and tell her about its effect on me. So when the after-performance chatter and ado faded, I walked up the stairs to stage level, entered a large door and, subsequently, a labyrinth of hallways. Her dressing room was surprisingly easy to find, marked with a large yellow star; and the door was half-open. I peeked inside before entering, but it was empty.

A woman with a hive of raven hair walked into the dressing room just as I was picking up one of Caroline's stockings. The woman told me in whispered tones to please leave the area, that the mistress had already retired to her house. I'd missed her. Fortunately, she said, I could make an appointment with the mistress for the following night if I paid £7000 to her immediately – in cash or jewels.

What? I exclaimed. Does it cost *that much* for a chat?

The woman laughed.

Then what are you interested in the mistress *for*, sir? She never speaks to anyone.

I know. She sings.

Ah, she said. I sense you are not like the others.

Then, perhaps out of pity, she told me where to find Caroline, without taking any money – which I would not have given her anyway.

The following evening, on my way to her home, I heard the sound of snow falling down slowly from a great height and shivered.

When I arrived the maid kindly let me in and led me to the parlour.

You may go in, she said. The mistress is expecting you.

I cracked open the door and peered inside the room. Caroline sat on a stool in front of a grand piano, her back towards me. I was shocked by the paleness of her skin against the wall's dark red wallpaper. Suddenly, as if she knew I was watching, there was a burst of music, which I recognized immediately as Chopin, a Polonaise I loved personally; and it lured me from the doorway into the room.

I approached her from behind, listening as the introduction of the piece rose with sweep and energy; a piece I had heard many times before but which was now speaking an entirely different language, audacious and original. Her body twisted and her billowing, black skirt rocked as she pressed her feet on the pedals. The rich harmonic web with its vigorous measures was closely woven, but not thick or heavy. I was quiet and worshipful as the notes entered into me and worked wonders on my imagination. I waited patiently, then there it was: the long, ever-increasing trill in one, two, three, four parts over a pedal-note, just after the intermezzo. She moved her arms with tremendous energy, as beads of sweat trapped her long hair at her neck. *She is like a landscape seen from a fast-moving train*, I thought. *Men would die for her and probably have already*. I walked around the piano to face her.

She did not look up but a coy smile spread across her beautiful face. The blue veins in her hands entranced me as her fingers carried the music to a climax then allowed it to fall away with a final loud chord that broke the spell. Suddenly, she stood up, and as she did, the comb in her hair loosened and skidded across the marble floor.

Oh no, she said softly.

I craned my head, wanting to hear her again, the bird. She was silent.

Here, let me help you with that, I said, and pulled a cream-colored, polka-dotted handkerchief out of my pocket.

Our eyes met briefly before hers dropped modestly.

Turn around.

She looked at me but didn't move.

Trust me, I said. Please.

She pivoted on her tiptoes. So I took her long fair hair in my hands, carefully gathered it at her neck and secured it with the handkerchief.

. . . And then I realized, as my friend finished telling this story, he was no longer seated and was standing behind me. He took my long fair hair in his hands, carefully gathered it at my neck and secured it with a handkerchief.

Do you still love her? I asked.

Yes, he said. But she's dead now.

An old photograph of a Swiss boy

Let me tell you how I discovered alchemy, he said, the third-to-the-last time I saw him, in Reykjavik, dining on *svið* (boiled sheep's head), *blóðmör* (blood sausage) and a sweet yoghurt known as *skyr,* made from curded milk. He handed me a black-n-white, postcard-sized photograph, which he extracted from his pocket.

That's me. He pointed to the photograph at a crowd of skiers in the snow that looked more like a swarm of mosquitoes on sugar. That's me: the insignificant one in the back.

You're so small, I said.

Well . . . he said, and fidgeted in his chair. It was taken in Gstaad, Switzerland, where I grew up, during my first downhill skiing class with a group of other boys. After the first snowfall of the season, usually in November, as I recall, we would hit the slopes and remain there until April.

He laughed.

What is so funny? I asked.

Oh . . . If you could have seen us: we flew down those mountain slopes at the speed of an express train!

I laughed and took another spoonful of *skyr*.

After an entire day of this up-n-down, up-n-down, we would retire to the lodge where we drank tea and ate honey out of pots with our fingers. We passed the pot around, reluctantly, each boy dipping in greedily. The taste was clean and sweet, like this *skyr*, as I recall, but light and mild, so we could continue to eat it for the better part of the evening without getting enough.

I was so enthralled with this delicate flavor as a boy that, even as an adult, it would not take leave of me. I was determined to uncover its source – and its entire evolution, for that matter.

After staying in London for many years, I returned to Gstaad in the early 1980s to undertake this research. I inspected the Swiss bees and tasted the honey over and over. I discovered its source: the nectar of the alpine rose, or *Rhododendron ferrugineum*, a shrub that grows throughout the higher Alps, the Pyrenees and the Apennines. Suddenly I found myself fascinated with honey-hunting, beekeeping, extracting and harvesting. I studied crystallization, hydrometry, density and relative density, viscosity, thixotropy, mutarotation, hygroscopicity, fermentation and labelling, all which led to my interest in the *quinta essentia*.

Which you believe is the life spirit of things, I said.

Yes, he replied. Every substance, like honey, has its own nature and energy which exist in the physical realm as well as the spiritual, emotional and mental realms. So as I learned how the properties of honey behaved physically, in my hands, I could experience the same energies at play within other dimensions, in my head.

So, I inquired, how did you get from bees to ice crystals?

Strangely enough, bees teach us the preoccupations of nature and the organization of life. For many, many years they have built their combs by linking the sciences with art. Yet, the entire process is mysterious. It took me a long time to uncover what is called "the spirit of the hive." Then, once I knew the source and the path of the original substance — the thing which started it all — I felt a profound sense of loss. And now I am no longer the eager young lad who can dip his finger into the syrup then thrust it in my mouth, enjoying it for the first time, encountering something *wholesome*. I know too much. My senses have been dulled so that I no longer feel that simultaneous desire for, and fear of, something completely foreign to me. I suppose it is that way with everything now — similar to the feeling one sometimes has after losing one's virginity.

Yes, I suppose, I said. But it doesn't have to be that way.

I know, my dear.

It isn't that way with snow, is it?
You tell me.*

A vial of perfume containing a scent that reminded him of his dead wife

As I told you, her name was Caroline — and I associate her scent with every love, longing and sadness there is in the world.

We sat in a café in Vienna, the fourth-to-the-last time I saw him, having enjoyed an Austrian feast of *wiener schnitzel* (breaded thin filet of veal), *paprikahändel* (paprika chicken), *hasenjunges* (offal of hare) and *knödelen* (dumplings), when he next said to me:

She used to put perfume on her lips before she kissed me.
Oh? Like Cleopatra.
Yes.
He extracted a vial from his bag and handed it to me.

---

* Hermes Trismegistos, father of Western alchemy, writes in *The Book of Seven Chapters*: "See, I have opened unto you what was hid: the work is with you and amongst you; in that it is to be found within you and is enduring; you will always have it present, wherever you are, on land or on sea." Herman von Helmholtz said in Frankfurt, 1865, during a lecture on ice and glaciers: "The world of ice and of eternal snow, as unfolded to us on the summits of the neighbouring Alpine chain, so stern, so solitary, so dangerous, it may be, has yet its own peculiar charm."

May I? I asked.

Please. Go ahead.

I removed the stopper, lifted the vial to my nose and inhaled.

Well, it's nice, I said. Fresh, spicy, woody.

You're not really *smelling* it, he said. Take a whiff and try to determine the quality and personality of the essence – its note, its form, what it suggests, like you would do when listening to a symphony or admiring a painting.

I can't.

Smell it again.

I lifted the vial to my nose.

Now I'll talk you through my own experience,* he said. While I rarely smell it, on the occasions that I do, this fragrance pervades my memory and immediately transports me to another place and time – to that hidden world which I reserve only for her. One whiff or drop feels like a reunion with the first scent in my life, the odor of my mother's milk. But as the fragrance wears on, its shifting nuances materialize gradually, like musical sounds, and their identities become harmonious.

The first notes are usually fresh and spicy like *nutmeg* and *black pepper*. Next I am hit with the base notes: *jojoba*

---

* "I will tell you of a perfume which my mistress has from the graces and the gods of love; when you smell it, you will ask of the deities to make of you only a nose." – Catullus.

oil and *civet* prowling through undertones of *costus* and *ambrette*, equally tenacious and primal. Initially this chord strikes me as offensive but gradually it becomes enticing, as aged brandy. I capture the sweet notes of *jasmine*, rich and warm, *orange flower absolute*, frisky and intense, and *tuberose,* sensual and volatile – all of which erase time to bring back the *first woman* and her timeless beauty.

Then I am moved to stir in, from memory, the distinctive smell of her body, which has been trapped in my nostrils for many years: the aroma of her unbound hair, her skin, breath and blood.

Finally, I uncover her sex, mysterious like the flower of the red-water rose, and its odor, like the muskiness of fur. The discreet emanation of her carries the perfume of honey or the sap of a maple – an aroma so persistent and steadfast that it drowns years . . . Its language makes my past remain present to me.

Let it go, I said.

I am. Take it.

I tucked the vial in my rucksack.

A journal, tied-up with string

Sunday, December 10, 2000

This morning, near the steps that descended twenty feet below into Liverpool Street station, a man leaned against a pillar and watched me closely. The first thing I noticed about him was the large scar that began at his right eyebrow, traveled down his face and disappeared beneath his beard. He stood so near I could feel his breath on my cheek and smell the long months of hunger and emptiness rising from his stomach, as he yelled in the cold with heavy puffs, "Go to hell, you bastards!" Passers-by, moving in great tides, ignored him, too intent on catching their 8:25 a.m. I knew they would blame him for ruining their day, later when they rode their big trains with their big faces. He would turn into that one irritation, however minor or brief, which made the day *so much* worse. My fingers fished for the newly purchased pack of cigarettes at the bottom of my rucksack. Once in my hands, I slipped the cellophane skin off and plucked the gold foil, revealing tight rows and white circles. "You're all bastards, I tell you!"

As I lit my own cigarette, a passer-by dropped a still-smoking one on the pavement. The man quickly snatched the butt from the ground, put it in his mouth and inhaled with closed eyes: his first or his last. I spied him and wondered how long he had gone without. The man exhaled slowly, and with one more pull his second-hand cigarette took its last breath. He looked straight at me so I glanced away, and became frighteningly aware of my own cigarette, the one that still burned strong between my fingers and suddenly felt much heavier. An unfamiliar guilt seized me – over *having, enjoying* – and this feeling revealed itself, no matter how I attempted to hide it, when my long cigarette trembled momentarily on my lips, and a piece of ash tumbled to the ground, scurrying along the pavement without breaking up. He saw it all, watching me. "Bastards!"

Of course there were more . . . the nearly full pack tucked in my rucksack. The man's badger-eyes focused on my bag, ravenous, and mentally shuffled through its contents, looking for *that one thing*: a key, a handkerchief, a photograph, a vial, a journal. No, no, no, no, no. He did not care about an iron key; a cream-colored, polka-dotted handkerchief; an old photograph of a Swiss boy; a vial of perfume containing a scent that reminded him of his dead wife; nor a journal, tied-up with string. He was only after those smokes – a desire so powerful his leg shook, reminiscent of my old spaniel. I frowned in a kind of heartache, then looked at my watch: five minutes for an espresso. Tugging at the straps of my rucksack so it hugged my back, I approached the entrance to the underworld without acknowledging the man, without goodbye. He did say something to me, but I couldn't hear him – the words were muffled as I reluctantly joined the masses and descended the stairs.

My train departed five minutes later.

Icy conditions on the platform, next station Colchester. Riding from Liverpool Street to Norwich the sun filtered through painterly clouds, pink and reaching down to the horizon. The sky, a chilling blue, emphasized the sheen of the white landscape and the glowing silence of the snow, but lingered too close – an uninvited intimacy. I was startled by the beauty around me and was forced to look back inside the train for some distance. My palms beaded with perspiration. Glancing around I noticed that everyone else seemed unaffected, but I could not decide if I was the lone witness or the single one left out. Perhaps these members of a foreign species – who chatted on mobile phones, read newspapers or engaged their neighbor in conversation; were, in the process, missing out on beauty surrounding them, and looking only at themselves – made me the lone witness. On the other hand, I was trapped inside another world, suspended in time – never touched a newspaper or spoke to a friend – as these people were both collectively and singularly engaged in acts of communication, as informers and receivers – which made me the single one left out.

Next station Ipswich. Tree after tree, stripped bare and beautiful, scraped the sides of the train and I flinched. I looked hard at my reflection in the window, catching now and again great flashes of white and blue snow in the twilight. My senses played tricks on me. I smelled, touched, tasted, heard and saw things, like his beautiful face next to me in the snowflakes that began to fall from the sky. I saw his blond curls, pale blue eyes and sardonic smile; heard the crackling sound of his tongue touching his teeth; felt his hand in mine – all the things that made him belong beside me. Eventually I no longer saw myself in the window,* for my cheek had become his cheek, my chin his chin. I reached out for his face, trailed my finger down the bridge of his nose and traced his lips.

It's not often one meets a great man.

These sensations overwhelmed me, brought me to tears and near-hysteria. Questions came – sometimes new, other times old, rewritten or rephrased – but with answers always out of reach. There is a child-boy-man, I thought, who lives his life in secrets wrapped around him like the skins of an onion; so how far can I peel and can I peel too far? Will I, equally onion-like, I wondered, lose my core in a pile of discarded husks?

And the more I wondered, the more I suspected that such knowledge was being withheld from me for *having, enjoying,* and never giving my cigarettes to that man outside the station. Or was that man simply becoming to me what he was to everyone else – the primary irritation of the day, the thing to blame for not knowing? Nothing came of these queries, but the whole brew of them was a poison intent on killing me slowly. *They're all bastards, I tell you.*

---

* Plato's myth describes original human beings as round, with their back and sides forming a circle, and having four arms and four legs. But the gods, who felt threatened by these beings, cut each of them in half. Ever since, each "half" has been wandering around, longing to be reunited with their "other half."

Next stop Norwich. It was snowing heavily and I thought, oh no, perhaps he is indoors and missing this miracle, the one man who loves Snow more than anything, who calls it "forgetful," and closes himself off in a laboratory in a bizarre celebration of it. The obsession began, he told me, when he would cross-country ski to school in the Bernese Alps. With their cones and crevices edged with snow, he said the mountains reminded him of Fujiyama, the dead volcano whose simple form you saw in Japanese paintings; among other things he said, which I could not remember; along with those questions, of course, one after another.

But if emotions are intimate perceptions of *bodily* changes that occur when one is in love, I thought, then perhaps the sweating, the tears had *caused* my fear and sense of confusion, not the other way round. In that case, if I could simply keep my body from reacting I could keep my heart and mind intact.

So I thought.

After I arrived at the station in Norwich, I took a taxi to the guesthouse. The manager greeted me and handed me a note that, she said, a young woman who wished to remain anonymous, had left for me. I opened it quickly, expecting *anything else*. It said: *Read today's newspaper*. I found nothing special in the handwriting, nothing compelling in the childlike script, and therefore wanted to resist following this direction. If not for the fact that the writer remained anonymous, I would have resisted. So, after the manager of the guesthouse handed me a key, I ascended the steep stairs and arrived at my designated room on the third floor, where I unloaded my belongings. Then I exited, locked the door, descended two stories, departed from the guesthouse and commenced my search for an American newspaper. How I knew where to look and what I was looking for remain a mystery; but I went from shop to shop until I found the *New York Times* in a newsstand and, after purchasing it, tucked it under my arm, where it remained undisturbed for the duration of my walk.

It took twenty minutes to return to the guesthouse.

Monday, December 11, 2000

I did not look at the newspaper last night, not until early this morning, after I had a night's rest, bathed and dressed, before descending the stairs once more. At the top of the staircase, just outside my room, I contemplated my actions. What will he say when I mysteriously show up on his doorstep, after coming all this way? Suddenly I felt the urge to open the newspaper, there and then. Leafing through the pages swiftly — 1,2,3,4 — not knowing what to look for, I caught the cruel image of a car twisted and tangled up, wrestling with a truck in the snow; and if I looked quite closely, a few haphazard specks of red on white. I felt dizzy. The article reported that a man died in a head-on collision

in Buffalo on Sunday . . . was pronounced dead at the scene
. . . Police not naming the casualty until relatives have been
informed. *The casualty*. An unidentified man that I knew was
him. I did not know he was coming to me in New York as I
was coming to him in England, but it almost made sense.
My head spun.

The last time I saw him – either weeks ago or a century,
I don't recall – I had visited his laboratory in Switzerland
and given him a little box wrapped in crinkled cream paper.

Why do you buy me things? he asked, frowning.

His lacklustre stung me. I hated when he distanced us,
so moved toward the door.

Tell me . . . How are you doing? he said, meaning, *Come
back*.

I looked over my shoulder at him opening the box and
pulling out the surprise, a brass compass – from WWII –
with a mother-of-pearl face.*

It's for your travels, I said, to keep you from getting lost.

How did you know? he asked, the compass in his palm.

---

* The compass is associated with truth and, according to Masonic
rituals, represents the balance between mind and matter. It is also a
symbol of duality and its transcendence: as one hand remains station-
ary in the center, the other forms a complete circle. According to Jung,
the compass represents an image of Self. Compasses are often associated with long and difficult journeys and, symbolically, can assist a
descent into the Underworld, where the traveller may find the center
of things, the *quinta essentia*, later returning to consciousness or reality.

He handled it for a moment and grinned as much as I'd ever seen.

I didn't know, I said.

Don't worry.

He then reached into his pocket and extracted a key, which he handed to me.

Take this and tuck it away in a safe place. It opens the door to my laboratory as well as the door to my study. Do you see?

Yes, I said, okay.

He sat back in his chair.

But why me? I asked.

That is very difficult to answer, he said.

What am I looking for?

Well, I don't know what all this means, he said. It's a completely random process, *this knowing* or not knowing . . . an unfathomable thing. The thought will simply arrive unexpectedly, I think, like you have been hit over the head.

Tell me.

Well, that is not important right now, he said, and looked out the window.

I frowned.

You ask a lot of questions.

He placed his cold hand on my cheek.

I remembered this moment, saw it very clearly, standing near the top of the stairs that descended two stories to the ground floor of the guesthouse; and I turned, knowing I had

to get out of there – run, go somewhere – but still clutching the paper, stepped down and lost my balance, stumbled
over my own foot at the top of the stairs, clutched the paper
tighter, tumbled headfirst, down-down, two flights and
trying to save the paper, hit the ground hard with a quake –
and then sprawled there, twisted up in the silence of the
hallway.

Or . . .

Perhaps it didn't happen that way at all.

Perhaps time came to a fork in the road, a Cartesian split,
immediately after I left the man coveting my cigarettes near
the steps that descended twenty feet below into Liverpool
Street station.

Perhaps after I had tumbled to the bottom of the staircase, I rose from my fall, brushed myself off and found
myself standing in the light that filtered through the glass
roof of the main hall of the station.

Perhaps I never made a journey at all.

And something else: I was urged to go back. Some
unknown force encircled me, guiding me up the stairs that
ascended to street level, toward the man who leaned against
the pillar, who really was still there. I reached into my rucksack, pulled out the pack of cigarettes and handed them over
with a grimace. When I looked up, his eyes met mine and,
following a salute, he shuffled away quickly.

I sighed in a kind of heartache and leaned against the
pillar, where the man had been, just outside the station,

near the steps that descended twenty feet below into the underworld. The wind wrapped around me, causing a shiver. Suddenly a newspaper fluttered nearby. I reached out, following it until the wind let up, allowing me to snatch it. The wrinkled pages fluttered in my hands as I flipped and searched. Inside, the cruel image: the mangled car and the blizzard, the phrase: unidentified man, the word: casualty. I felt a great anger surge through me but didn't know whom to blame. "You're all bastards," I yelled in the cold.

. . . But the day of the discovery is unimportant – today or yesterday's news – so is the stumbling place – the stairs at Liverpool Street station or the guesthouse in Norwich. The important thing is: I had been hit over the head.

Tuesday, December 12, 2000

Inside the rucksack I found the key.
Inside the laboratory I found the study.
Inside the desk I found the book of solutions.

And it is found in every place and at any time and in every circumstance, when the search lies heavy on the searcher.

Petronius

OTHER PICADOR BOOKS

AVAILABLE FROM PAN MACMILLAN

PATRICIA DUNCKER

JAMES MIRANDA BARRY	0 330 37169 X	£6.99
THE DEADLY SPACE BETWEEN	0 330 49010 9	£6.99
SEVEN TALES OF SEX AND DEATH	0 330 49011 7	£16.99

HOWARD NORMAN

THE MUSEUM GUARD	0 330 37010 3	£6.99
THE HAUNTING OF L	0 330 37225 4	£15.99

CLAIRE MESSUD

WHEN THE WORLD WAS STEADY	0 330 48817 1	£6.99
THE HUNTERS	0 330 48815 5	£6.99

All Pan Macmillan titles can be ordered from our website,
www.panmacmillan.com, or from your local bookshop
and are also available by post from:

Bookpost, PO Box 29, Douglas, Isle of Man IM99 1BQ
Credit cards accepted. For details:
Telephone: 01624 677237
Fax: 01624 670923
E-mail: bookshop@enterprise.net
www.bookpost.co.uk

Free postage and packing in the United Kingdom

Prices shown above were correct at the time of going to press.
Pan Macmillan reserve the right to show new retail prices on covers
which may differ from those previously advertised in the text
or elsewhere.